WRECK THE HALLS

A WORST DETECTIVE EVER CHRISTMAS
NOVELLA, BOOK 9

CHRISTY BARRITT

River Heights

COMPLETE BOOK LIST

Squeaky Clean Mysteries:

#1 Hazardous Duty

#2 Suspicious Minds

#2.5 It Came Upon a Midnight Crime (novella)

#3 Organized Grime

#4 Dirty Deeds

#5 The Scum of All Fears

#6 To Love, Honor and Perish

#7 Mucky Streak

#8 Foul Play

#9 Broom & Gloom

#10 Dust and Obey

#11 Thrill Squeaker

#11.5 Swept Away (novella)

#12 Cunning Attractions

#13 Cold Case: Clean Getaway

#14 Cold Case: Clean Sweep

#15 Cold Case: Clean Break

#16 Cleans to an End

While You Were Sweeping, A Riley Thomas Spinoff

The Sierra Files:

#1 Pounced

#2 Hunted

#3 Pranced

#4 Rattled

The Gabby St. Claire Diaries (a Tween Mystery series):

#1 The Curtain Call Caper

#2 The Disappearing Dog Dilemma

#3 The Bungled Bike Burglaries

The Worst Detective Ever

#1 Ready to Fumble

#2 Reign of Error

#3 Safety in Blunders

#4 Join the Flub

#5 Blooper Freak

#6 Flaw Abiding Citizen

#7 Gaffe Out Loud

#8 Joke and Dagger

#9 Wreck the Halls
#10 Glitch and Famous
#11 Not on My Botch

Raven Remington
Relentless

Holly Anna Paladin Mysteries:
#1 Random Acts of Murder
#2 Random Acts of Deceit
#2.5 Random Acts of Scrooge
#3 Random Acts of Malice
#4 Random Acts of Greed
#5 Random Acts of Fraud
#6 Random Acts of Outrage
#7 Random Acts of Iniquity

Lantern Beach Mysteries
#1 Hidden Currents
#2 Flood Watch
#3 Storm Surge
#4 Dangerous Waters
#5 Perilous Riptide
#6 Deadly Undertow

Lantern Beach Romantic Suspense
#1 Tides of Deception

#2 Shadow of Intrigue

#3 Storm of Doubt

#4 Winds of Danger

#5 Rains of Remorse

#6 Torrents of Fear

Lantern Beach P.D.

#1 On the Lookout

#2 Attempt to Locate

#3 First Degree Murder

#4 Dead on Arrival

#5 Plan of Action

Lantern Beach Escape

Afterglow (a novelette)

Lantern Beach Blackout

#1 Dark Water

#2 Safe Harbor

#3 Ripple Effect

#4 Rising Tide

Lantern Beach Guardians

#1 Hide and Seek

#2 Shock and Awe

#3 Safe and Sound

Lantern Beach Blackout: The New Recruits

#1 Rocco

#2 Axel

#3 Beckett

#4 Gabe

Lantern Beach Mayday

#1 Run Aground

#2 Dead Reckoning

#3 Tipping Point

Lantern Beach Blackout: Danger Rising

#1 Brandon

#2 Dylan

#3 Maddox

#4 Titus

Lantern Beach Christmas

Silent Night

Crime á la Mode

#1 Dead Man's Float

#2 Milkshake Up

#3 Bomb Pop Threat

#4 Banana Split Personalities

Beach Bound Books and Beans Mysteries

#1 Bound by Murder

#2 Bound by Disaster

#3 Bound by Mystery

#4 Bound by Trouble

#5 Bound by Mayhem

Vanishing Ranch

#1 Forgotten Secrets

#2 Necessary Risk

#3 Risky Ambition

#4 Deadly Intent

#5 Lethal Betrayal

#6 High Stakes Deception

#7 Fatal Vendetta

#8 Troubled Tidings

#9 Narrow Escape

The Sidekick's Survival Guide

#1 The Art of Eavesdropping

#2 The Perks of Meddling

#3 The Exercise of Interfering

#4 The Practice of Prying

#5 The Skill of Snooping

#6 The Craft of Being Covert

Saltwater Cowboys

#1 Saltwater Cowboy

#2 Breakwater Protector

#3 Cape Corral Keeper

#4 Seagrass Secrets

#5 Driftwood Danger

#6 Unwavering Security

Beach House Mysteries

#1 The Cottage on Ghost Lane

#2 The Inn on Hanging Hill

#3 The House on Dagger Point

School of Hard Rocks Mysteries

#1 The Treble with Murder

#2 Crime Strikes a Chord

#3 Tone Death

Carolina Moon Series

#1 Home Before Dark

#2 Gone By Dark

#3 Wait Until Dark

#4 Light the Dark

#5 Taken By Dark

Suburban Sleuth Mysteries:

Death of the Couch Potato's Wife

Fog Lake Suspense:

#1 Edge of Peril

#2 Margin of Error

#3 Brink of Danger

#4 Line of Duty

#5 Legacy of Lies

#6 Secrets of Shame

#7 Refuge of Redemption

Cape Thomas Series:

#1 Dubiosity

#2 Disillusioned

#3 Distorted

Standalone Romantic Mystery:

The Good Girl

Suspense:

Imperfect

The Wrecking

Sweet Christmas Novella:

Home to Chestnut Grove

Standalone Romantic-Suspense:

Keeping Guard

The Last Target

Race Against Time

Ricochet

Key Witness

Lifeline

High-Stakes Holiday Reunion

Desperate Measures

Hidden Agenda

Mountain Hideaway

Dark Harbor

Shadow of Suspicion

The Baby Assignment

The Cradle Conspiracy

Trained to Defend

Mountain Survival

Dangerous Mountain Rescue

Nonfiction:

Characters in the Kitchen

Changed: True Stories of Finding God through Christian Music (out of print)

The Novel in Me: The Beginner's Guide to Writing and Publishing a Novel (out of print)

CHAPTER ONE

"WHAT'S this show you're guest hosting called again?" Jackson Sullivan crossed his arms and leaned against his police SUV. It was parked in the driveway outside a rental home as we waited for a caravan of vehicles to meet us.

I pulled my winter white coat closer as a frigid wind came over the ocean and spread its icy fingers over the sandy landscape—and over me. "It's called *Lit*."

He squinted, looking unaffected by the cold—unlike me as I danced and jumped around to stay warm. "Doesn't that mean drunk?"

"It *used* to mean drunk. Now, in the current vernacular, it means excited or hyped." I positioned my hands into peace signs, mimicking every Instagrammer out there, and even added duck lips. "You know, as in, that party was *lit*."

Jackson grunted as if he still didn't believe me. Or like he thought I'd lost it. Maybe both.

"Anyway, *Lit* is a TV special that will feature some of the best decorated homes in the country at Christmastime," I said. "The families chosen to have their houses featured will also have money donated to a charity on their behalf."

"Sounds noble."

"It is. And fun. And festive. And all that's merry and bright!"

"Kind of like you."

"You're so sweet that I could marry you." I stepped closer and grabbed the scarf around Jackson's neck. I'd given the red cashmere piece to him myself and thought it looked nice with his black leather jacket. I tugged him closer to me. "It's going to be a great show."

A smile started at the corner of Jackson's lips. "Is it?"

"Yes. You're going to love it." I continued pulling him closer until I was able to plant a kiss on his lips. "I'm so glad my friend talked me into hosting it with her."

Only five more months and I would be able to call this man my husband. I couldn't wait. We still had so much wedding planning to do, though. At least we'd been having fun picking everything out lately. We'd tasted cakes, sampled menus, checked out potential honeymoon spots. It was the perfect way to spend my time off work.

"At least I'll get to have you here and all to myself for the next month," Jackson murmured, wrapping his arms around my waist.

"Exactly. Except for this week. This week, we'll film *Lit*. I have a couple of press opportunities, a charity dinner, and the Christmas parade."

"Is that all?" He raised his eyebrows, his words dryly sarcastic.

I shrugged. "That's it. And you get to act as my personal security. Thank you, Mayor Allen."

"Whatever I can do to serve my city."

I was about to flirt some more when three SUVs pulled into the driveway. The crew had arrived. I stepped away from Jackson, trying not to be one of those PDA couples, but I instantly missed his warmth.

Now that the crew had arrived, we only had an hour to debrief and go over all the details before we headed over to the filming site. Our schedule would be tight, but this was going to be fun.

Especially because . . .

"Starla!" I let out a squeal as my friend's head

appeared out of the back door of the black Expedition.

It had been so long since I'd seen my best friend. So. Long. And I missed her like Scooby would miss Shaggy, or Thelma would miss Louise. I mean, not enough to drive my car off a cliff but . . . you get the drift.

She hopped out and ran toward me, a matching squeal escaping from her. "Joey Darling! I can't believe we're finally seeing each other!"

"It's been too long."

We hugged, kissed each other's cheeks, and squealed some more. We were totally cliché BFFs, and I didn't even care.

I stepped back, still squeezing her arms, and studied my friend. She looked different since I'd last seen her. "Your hair!"

She was known for her long, luxurious blonde locks. But her new do was short, honey blonde, and almost boyish.

"It's for a new role in the *Gladiator Diaries*," she said. "Did I tell you I got the lead role in that one?"

I twisted my head. This was the first I'd heard of it. "The movie with Dwayne 'The Rock' Johnson? No, I had no idea."

"Totally. It's like the *Gladiator* meets *The Princess*

Diaries. My agent thinks it will be a smashing success."

"Sounds like quite the combination." How could it not be?

Memories of my last movie floated back to me. It had been like James Bond meets *Driving Miss Daisy*, and I still thanked God every day it had fallen through. But that was just me.

"It is. Anyway, the director asked me to cut my hair for the role." She reached for the nape of her neck and rubbed her hand there, looking uncertain. "I didn't want to do something this extreme, but I did it anyway. I decided to take one for the team."

"It's cute." Starla would look good if she shaved her head bald. She was that type of person—tiny and perky with delicate features. Sometimes she could be a bit of an airhead, but it was in an endearing way. Besides, she was a ton of fun to be around.

"Thanks, girlfriend." She looped her arm through mine. "Now, are you ready to do this Christmas special?"

"Ready as Rudolph on Christmas Eve."

As the rest of the crew scrambled around us to move their things inside, Starla's gaze drifted over my shoulder, and her smile brightened. "You must be the Hubba Hubba Hunka Hunka Jackson."

"Oh, I'm so sorry." I shrugged with overly dramatic guilt and maybe even a little embarrassment over her word choice. "I forgot to introduce you!"

Jackson stepped toward her and extended his hand. "Nice to meet you."

"Oh, it's even nicer to meet you," Starla gushed. "I've heard so much about you. All good. Apparently, you put every hero on every TV show to shame."

"I don't know if I'd say *that*." He shrugged, always humble when he had every reason to be cocky. Maybe not *always* humble and *never* cocky, but close enough.

"I *would* say that. Joey would *never* exaggerate." Starla grinned, looking as charming as always as she elbowed me. "I have no reason to doubt her."

I took Starla's arm before she embarrassed Jackson anymore. We needed a subject change. "Are you ready for this?"

"Are you kidding? This is going to make our star power rise. You know what that means? Cha-ching!"

I smiled while inwardly cringing. She reminded me so much of my old life. The life I'd tried to leave behind. For the most part, I had for almost the past year.

But I didn't want to be the kind of person who sought after tabloid exposure or who acted crazy just for more press time. I hoped my time around Starla wouldn't push me back into my old ways.

No, it wouldn't. I was stronger than that. Life and experience had changed me.

I decided to change the subject. "So, is Thompson here?"

Thompson Aims was the producer of this show. *Lit* had been filmed in seven different locations so far, and different celebrities had hosted each place. Now, it was our turn here in Nags Head, North Carolina. Starla and I were the last to film.

Christmas was only four weeks away, so our episode would air right before Christmas day. The show would not only highlight families and towns, but also charities and small-town traditions. All in all, it was a win-win-win!

"I think I saw Thompson scurry past," Starla said. "I know he wants to explain to us how everything will go down this week."

"Makes sense."

"Have I ever told you just how much I *love* Christmas? This whole experience is going to be the *bomb*."

The bomb . . . lit . . . I was seeing a theme here.

Explosions.

I only hoped that the explosion was of the good variety . . . an explosion of love and giving and peace on earth.

Because in my experience, explosions meant danger and crime and being chased by bad guys.

Over the next hour, Thompson debriefed Starla and me on how everything would go down today. What the process would be. How much time we had.

Jackson had also met with Thompson to run through how things would go tonight. They'd expected big crowds, which meant a police presence was needed.

After that, Starla and I went to hair and makeup. As much as I loved the end result of hair and makeup, I hated the process. Looking good wasn't easy.

But finally, I was done. Thankfully, the show had provided us everything we needed, as Starla's luggage had apparently gotten lost at the airport.

I'd been clothed in black leggings with a white tunic top, an adorable black leather jacket, and a green and red plaid scarf. Starla had been assigned a coordinating outfit of white leggings, a green tunic, and a maroon-colored duster sweater.

Finally, we were set.

Jackson would come with us as part of a security detail. You know, just in case. Because in my world, just in cases happened all the time. So Jackson had insisted on being present . . . wait for it . . . *just in case.*

The mayor of Nags Head was on board for all of this because he wanted as much positive press for the area as he could possibly get, especially now that he was running for senator. The election was still a year away, but he was in full campaign mode.

That led Starla and I up to this moment: the moment when we were ready for show time.

Our caravan of SUVs pulled into a little neighborhood on the west side of the island. This was the area where full-timers were more likely to live—away from the ocean and the homes close to the shore where tourists flocked.

All kinds of different homes graced the hilly streets—traditionally stilted beach homes, brick ranches, and even some colonials. It was eclectic, but I liked eclectic. Several homes were decorated modestly for the upcoming holiday.

Before we even reached our destination, I could see the crowds had started to gather in the street.

This was going to be interesting.

It was only three in the afternoon. The real show wouldn't start until the sun went down at five or so. I felt confident everything would go according to plan, especially since Thompson Aims was at the helm.

The man was legendary for TV specials like this.

They were each heartwarming, fun, and feel-good. The man himself was on the quieter side. He had an affection for fedoras, which matched his chunky glasses and soft voice.

"So, you meet the family," Thompson said as we approached the house in the Expedition. "You hear their story. Then you tour their home and *ooh* and *ahh* over all their decorations. This is a kind show. No mean comments."

I was kind of appalled he even had to say that. As far as I knew, I didn't have a reputation of being a jerk . . . did I? "Of course."

He offered a brief shake of his head, as if realizing what he'd said. "You're going to do great. Yes, of course."

"Or our names aren't Starla and Joey." Starla hooked her arm and swung it, as if overacting in a vaudeville comedy show.

"Knock 'em dead, ladies," Thompson said.

He probably wouldn't have said that if he'd known just how many times I'd had near-death encounters since I'd moved to this sleepy little sandbar town. But he didn't, so I moved on.

We parked. Jackson had followed behind us in his official police SUV. I kind of felt like the president with all the dark SUVs and security detail. In a few minutes, when I donned the media darling side of my personality and began shaking hands with people, I might actually feel like I was running for election. My campaign slogan could be *All hail the goof.*

It had a nice ring to it, right?

As the camera crew set up their equipment and production put up a tent, Starla and I met the family, the Curriers.

Frank and Tammy were in their early fifties. Frank was robust—everything from his belly, to his nose, to his loud voice. Tammy had an eighties kind of style with her big brunette hair, bold makeup, and mom jeans. Then again, the eighties were coming back in fashion, so maybe she was smart to hold onto the style. The couple had a teenage boy named Fitz.

Their charity of choice was a local fire station. Frank had been a firefighter for twenty years until he recently retired. Unlike other shows, every family that was featured got money. In fact, a ticker would run at the bottom of the screen where viewers could also donate beyond the twenty thousand the show was kicking in.

As we continued to talk to them, we learned that the family had only moved here three years ago. However, they'd always loved decorating for Christmas. That fact was evident now.

A hodgepodge of decorations surrounded us,

from blow molds to wire-frame figures to anima-tronic animals. Christmas music blared from speak-ers, and a fake snow machine shot foamy flakes into the air.

A little gingerbread booth had been set up on the corner of the property, and two elementary-aged girls gave out hot chocolate and cookies. Neighbors gath-ered in the streets, wearing their Christmas best and chattering happily. I even saw a couple of people exchange gifts.

It was the picture of Christmas perfection.

I took a step away from the house and mingled with the crowds, offering high fives and autographs and sage pieces of wisdom like "Don't eat yellow snow" and "When in doubt, mumble."

As my gaze scanned the roofline, I spotted a sled with Santa and his elves inside, as well as eight rein-deer in front. The whole scene was illuminated by string lights. Stars had also been placed strategically around the roof.

My gaze stopped on the chimney, and I blinked, uncertain if I was seeing correctly. Everything else at the house seemed so uniform and purposeful but . . . one decoration seemed out of place amongst the rest.

I wandered over to the Curriers and pointed. "That's such a unique decoration . . . I love the way you put the naughty Santa getting stuck inside the chimney."

I actually found it odd, but I wanted to hear the story behind it. Two legs, clad in black, stuck up straight from the brick chimney.

Mrs. Currier's gaze jerked toward where I pointed, and she frowned.

"We didn't put Santa coming down into the chimney." Her face looked tense with confusion. "And a naughty Santa?" Her face went from confused to appalled. "That would be enough to cause nightmares for our smallest of visitors. We'd never do that. Mother wouldn't approve."

Guess I'd read that one wrong.

Starla, along with a cameraman, joined us.

Starla's eyelashes fluttered in confusion. "Then who do those two legs belong to?"

Mr. and Mrs. Currier exchanged a frown as they stood beside each other on the front lawn.

"I didn't put anything in the chimney," Mr. Currier said. "Did you?"

Mrs. Currier shook her head. "No, like I said, I would never want to scare children with something like that. It doesn't look festive. It looks like . . . " She swallowed hard. "Something from *The Nightmare Before Christmas*."

Starla and I exchanged a glance. I tried to keep

my expression neutral, especially since I knew the cameras were still rolling and capturing my every action.

"Maybe Fitz put something up there as a joke. Fitz!" Mr. Currier's voice boomed. "Come over here for a second!"

Their son wandered over. He was probably seventeen or eighteen, twenty pounds overweight, and had a buzz cut that did nothing to enhance his features.

When he looked at Starla, I could tell by the way his eyes brightened that he was crushing on her. He didn't have to say or do anything for that point to be clear. His eyes lit up like a little boy . . . wait for it . . . on Christmas day.

Man, I was good.

"Fitz." Mr. Currier's voice hardened. "Do you know anything about the legs in the chimney?"

Fitz pulled his gaze away from Starla for long enough to look on top of the roof. "Legs? In the chimney? Why would I do that? You know I hate heights."

"So you know nothing about this?" Mr. Currier's tone took on the tone of a stern father, all his Christmas cheer seeming to disappear. "You didn't put a mannequin up there as a joke? I know you wanted to do a dark humor Christmas theme."

Fitz pulled his gaze back over toward his father,

skimming Starla again as he did. "No, Father. I know nothing about that."

His voice sounded a little too saccharine. Was that because he was lying? Or was he just trying to get under his father's skin?

I looked back at Jackson at that moment. When I saw the frown on his face, I knew exactly what he was thinking—that I had found trouble . . . again.

And he may have been right.

But the only thing going through my mind was a re-written version of "Up on the Housetop." Except my lyrics went something like this:

Down through the chimney with lots of ploy.
Because that man's a Christmas decoy.

CHAPTER
TWO

WITH THE CAMERAS STILL ROLLING, a crew from the police department set up a ladder and climbed on top of the Curriers' house. Starla and I stood in the background, watching everything as it happened.

A terrible thought continued to run through my mind.

Those legs didn't look like they belonged to a mannequin.

Those legs looked real.

I could be wrong. It was all conjecture. But there was just something about them . . . about the white socks beneath the black pants. About the scuffed gray tennis shoes. About the leg hair that peeked out as gravity pulled the clothing downward.

But I was trying to wait and hear an official word

on things. I wouldn't jump to conclusions or assume the worst.

The Christmas music had been cut, my hot chocolate was now cold, and all of the jolly left as if the Grinch had come into town and personally stole it all.

Starla looped her arm through mine and pulled me closer as we watched.

"Is this what your life is always like?" she whispered, appearing slightly dumbstruck at the turn of events.

I wanted to deny it. I wanted to tell her that my life was nothing like this. But the truth was that, more often than not, this was *exactly* what my life was like.

Mysteries had a way of finding me. Hunting me down. Clobbering me over the head.

Here I thought we were going to do a simple Christmas special and that I would be able to enjoy the holidays afterward. But obviously that was not going to be the case.

That thought was confirmed when I saw the police officers pull the man from the chimney. His body looked stiff.

But it wasn't because he was a dummy. It was because of rigor mortis.

There was a time when I thought I'd only know

that phrase because I'd used it on my TV series, *Relentless*. But instead, I'd used the term in real life more times than I could count.

Starla held my arm tighter. "Joey . . . that was . . . a real dead body, wasn't it?"

I felt bad for my friend. I really did. I could remember the first time I had discovered my first real dead body too. It hadn't exactly been a fun or humorous moment.

No matter how many times you saw things like this on TV or how many times you acted in a movie where a dead body was found, there was a distinct difference between seeing one in real life and knowing one was fake on TV. Real dead bodies deserved a moment of mourning and respect.

"That man appears to be real," I murmured.

She turned toward me, her eyes wide. "Who do you think it is?"

I glanced at the Curriers. They looked equally as horrified, as did everyone else around us. I had a feeling they had no idea who he was either. If they did, their faces showed no recognition.

"I have no idea," I said. "What are the chances that someone would actually get stuck in a chimney at Christmastime? It seems so . . . twisted."

"Do you think this will make it on the air?" Starla nodded behind her to the camera crew.

Their eyes looked surprisingly hungry, like they knew a story like this would dominate news stations. Hollywood loved an interesting tale . . . and this definitely seemed like one.

Some of the crowds had wandered away by now as the night deepened. Thompson stood with the Curriers, his body language showing compassion as he bent toward them and reassuringly placed a hand on Mrs. Currier's shoulder. It was so great to work with someone with integrity.

But did the crew really have to keep filming?

"This isn't exactly the PR the show is going to want to get," I said. "They want to bring happy, warm, fuzzy feelings of Christmas and the holidays. Dead bodies don't generally do that to people. I think Thompson will agree."

Starla shivered. "Yeah, I know. I just don't understand why they're still filming."

"My guess is they'll sell this to an affiliate news station."

"Seems despicable."

"I'm sure they have ways of justifying it." *Business is business. News is news. Money dominates.*

They'd never say that last one, but it was true.

I straightened as Jackson wandered back over toward us. His face clearly showed that he was not happy. His eyes were narrowed and his body tense.

"Any updates that you're allowed to share?" I asked.

"No, there is nothing that I can share at this point. Mostly because there's nothing that we know yet. We need to get a better look at this guy."

"I don't suppose he carried a wallet in his pocket?" Starla's voice lilted with innocence.

"If only it was that easy." Jackson pressed his lips together.

I crossed my arms, feeling in my element—even if I totally wasn't. "Any idea how he died?"

"Truthfully? It looks like he climbed inside the chimney and got stuck."

"Do you mean he died like that? Stuck in a narrow chimney for who knows how long?" The thought seemed horrific.

"That's how it appears." Jackson glanced back at the house as if picturing how it all happened. "The family said the last time they were on their roof was yesterday morning. This man wasn't there then."

"I can't imagine dying that way." I shivered just thinking about it.

"That's one way I would not want to die," Jackson agreed.

My mind was already racing. How long would it take someone to die in that position? I really had no idea. No more than twenty-four hours, I supposed.

But they would have to be twenty-four terrible hours.

Hadn't anyone heard him scream? Heard him struggle? Why had no one seen him before?

I wasn't a medical examiner, nor had I ever played one on TV. But I couldn't wait to hear the final analysis on what had happened.

I watched as the police loaded the dead body onto a gurney. Carefully, they lowered him down onto the ground. The officers had set up a line around the perimeter of the Curriers' house, allowing no one except the police to enter the area.

Another police blockade had been set up at the front of the street. The last thing we needed right now was merry-goers trying to come past to see the lights, only to see a dead body instead. Talk about traumatic.

This whole thing had turned into more of a circus than I ever anticipated.

Jackson wandered over toward the victim and pulled the sheet back. As soon as I saw Jackson's face, I realized he'd recognized the man. He stepped back and said something to the other officers.

I held my breath. I couldn't wait to hear who this man was and how Jackson knew him.

And I was pretty sure that fact made me a Scrooge.

I had to be patient in order to get any answers. But I felt like I'd been at this house and waiting in limbo forever. As Thompson and the crew packed up, I'd done my best to distract people by signing autographs. Despite that, people had thrown out questions, and reporters had shown up.

What I really wanted to do was immerse myself in the middle of this investigation.

This was now a crime scene, and crime scene tape did not fit the Christmas decor we were looking for in order to make people's spirits a little brighter. The lights were now off, the sweet treats put away, and a general air of lethargy stretched where Christmas cheer had once reigned.

The coroner had taken the body away. John Doe would be examined to discover the true cause of death. Meanwhile, the CSI team was on the roof, gathering any evidence they could find on the man.

Finally, after what felt like hours, Jackson wandered back over toward me. My breath caught, and my blood seemed to sizzle at the sight of him.

Jackson always did that to my heart. I hoped that never changed and that he always got my pulse racing. My fingers were also crossed that he might be able to share something with me now.

Starla wandered away to talk to Thompson, leaving us alone for a moment.

"How's it going?" I asked. It sounded a little more simple than a diving right in with, *Can you tell me everything you know?*

My hunger for answers needed to be satisfied like an open fire needed chestnuts.

"It looks like it's going to be a long night." Jackson's breath frosted in front of him. "Every inch of this place is going to have to be scoured, and there are a lot of inches to this place when you take all these decorations into account."

I lowered my voice and stepped closer. "You recognized him, didn't you?"

His gaze darkened. "I put that man in jail about five years ago. His name was Christian Nolan."

I sucked in a breath. "So our victim was a criminal?"

And the plot thickens, my internal narrator said in a dramatic voice.

"He had been in jail? Why? Did he kill somebody?" Talk about the nightmare before Christmas . . .

"No, Nolan didn't kill anybody. He robbed several jewelry stores here in the area."

"He went to prison for five years for that?"

"That's right. He just got out three days ago."

I looked back at the Curriers' place, trying to put the pieces together. "Then what was this guy doing here?"

"That's what we're trying to figure out. Most likely, he was either drunk or high when this happened. It's the only thing that makes sense."

My mind continued to race. Since I couldn't jump in and question anyone, I'd just question Jackson instead. "Did the Curriers know him?"

"We don't know yet."

"Just one more question: how did the family not hear anything? Didn't the man scream? Struggle?"

"Apparently, they sleep with white noise— Christmas music right now. They didn't hear anything. Anyway, we'll be investigating all that we can. In fact, I'm probably going to be out late tonight. Do you have a ride home?"

"Are you sure we need to leave? I don't mind staying." Code: I want to stay and be nosy. I wanted to be in the middle of the action, living out my fake crime fighting persona.

Jackson gave me a knowing look. "I think it's for the best if you go."

"If you're sure. I know Thompson called a driver for us, someone with Ryderz." Ryderz was one of those ride services, kind of like Uber.

Jackson stepped closer and planted a kiss on my

cheek. "I am absolutely sure. You just get your beauty rest, and we'll figure everything out from here."

"Okay then." I tried to hide the disappointment from my voice.

I took a step away, but Jackson called my name. I paused and turned to him, my heart lifting with hope. Had he forgotten to share something?

"I guess this incident gives a whole new meaning to 'lit'."

CHAPTER
THREE

AS STARLA and I waited for our ride to arrive, Fitz wandered over to us. We were sitting in little camping chairs, with water and some trail mix next to us, under a tent that had been set up for the production crew.

Not surprisingly, Fitz's gaze was on Starla. "I just want to let you know I've loved you in every movie and TV show you've ever been in."

Starla smiled sweetly. "That's very kind of you. I always appreciate fans who are diehard like you."

"I think I've memorized almost every line of every movie."

Okay, now that was getting just a little bit creepy. I'd had my fair share of creepy encounters with overzealous fans in the past. More than I would like, for that matter.

Starla was the queen of knowing how to handle these situations. She could be kind yet firm, like she was born with an affinity for letting down guys gently. She'd certainly had enough experience.

"You even look pretty with that awful haircut."

Starla frowned and touched her hair again. "Thank you . . . I think."

Fitz beamed.

Starla's frown disappeared and she snapped into entertainer mode again. "Would you like my autograph?"

You would think she had just asked him if he wanted a date. He grinned from ear to ear. "Yes, I would love that. Let me grab something for you to sign . . . actually, I can't get inside to grab anything right now. Maybe tomorrow? I'm assuming you guys will be coming back here again?"

"That's my guess." Starla shrugged apologetically. "So how about if we take a rain check on that?"

"That sounds great." Fitz's face continued to light up like a Christmas tree. This guy was definitely taken with her, so much so that he could be one of those lawn ornaments that shone brightly.

Before we could talk anymore, a black sedan with a "Ryderz" sticker on the side window pulled up. Starla and I checked the license plate—just to be safe—and then climbed into the backseat.

She was going to stay at my house while she was here in town. It would only be for a few days, but a few days with Starla were better than no days with Starla.

Christmas was our favorite time of the year, so I couldn't wait to spend some of that time together. Plus, we both needed to catch up. She was one of my only true Hollywood friends.

She had been with me through thick and thin. And, when I said thick or thin, I meant through a bad marriage and a crashed career. Thank goodness things were finally getting back on track.

"An exciting night for you ladies," the driver said, glancing in the rearview mirror.

The man looked like an aging surfer with his graying blonde hair and premature wrinkles. He talked with a deep, slow drawl that made me think he'd spent too many days partying hard after catching waves.

"You can say that again," Starla muttered.

"I got here earlier but got stuck by the police barricade. I got out of the car to pass time, and some guy was asking about you two. Seemed oddly curious, you know?"

"What was he asking?" My mental radar for trouble began beeping.

The driver shrugged. "He said he wanted to impress you by making a statement."

"Impress who?" I clarified.

"He didn't specify which of you he was talking about."

"What did he look like?"

The driver shrugged again. "It was dark outside. He was tall with dark hair. I'm not sure what else I can tell you."

This was all . . . disturbing, to say the least. "You're going to need to tell the police this."

"All right, all right. If you think I should."

"You'll do that after you drop us off?"

"I'll go back and do it. Whatever I can do to help." He glanced back at us. "Didn't mean to upset you. How about if I turn on some Christmas music?"

I was grateful for his sensitivity. Mostly, I wanted time to sort out my thoughts on what had happened this evening.

A few minutes later, the driver dropped us off at my house. But even as I walked inside, my mind was on everything that had just transpired.

Why in the world had someone who'd just gotten out of jail managed to find himself stuck in a chimney at a local house that was known for its Christmas decorations and attention?

I told myself I wouldn't worry about it and that I

would continue on with life as normal, that I would continue to film the show, to spend time with Starla, and to squeeze in a few dates with my fiancé.

And, for the sake of all that was jolly and good in this world, that is what I would try to do.

————————

"So, I really like Jackson," Starla told me over coffee the next morning at my favorite place.

Sunrise Coffee Company had eclectic furniture, a resident tabby cat, and a golden doodle named Java. When I was at home, I loved coming to the café. They even had my favorite biscotti—cinnamon and sugar.

Starla and I had stolen a few minutes away so we could catch up. It seemed so stereotypical, but we'd both donned baseball hats and oversized sunglasses before leaving my house. We didn't want to be recognized, and this usually did the trick.

With the acoustic, folksy Christmas music playing overhead, we sipped our peppermint lattes and caught up.

I couldn't help but grin at Starla's words. *I really like Jackson.* "I know, right? Isn't he great? Seriously, I pinch myself every day when I think about how lucky I am to have met him."

I'd talked to him this morning to make sure the

Ryderz driver had talked to him. He had. Jackson had gotten a description of the man and would be looking into him more.

He'd warned me to stay away from this investigation. He'd seen me nearly lose my life one too many times, it appeared. So I'd told him I would. Thankfully, I had Starla to distract me, as well as a packed schedule.

"I can't wait to come back to this area again for your wedding," Starla continued. "It's just so beautiful here. I had no idea."

My fingers wrapped around my chunky, hand thrown coffee mug. "You should be here when it's not cold. It's even better."

"The beach on a cold day is still better than anywhere else."

"I agree." I leaned back in the vintage chair where I sat, settling in for some serious chitchat. "So, tell me about all of the new films you have coming up."

For the next hour, the two of us talked shop about Hollywood.

As soon as we finished our talk and our coffee, I glanced at my watch. "You know, I'm surprised we haven't heard from Thompson yet. Do you think he went back to the Currier house?"

"He could have."

"Maybe we should head out to the site and see if Thompson is there."

I had to admit, I had ulterior motives. Part of me wanted to go to the Curriers' just to see if there were any updates about what was going on.

I wanted to know how that man had gotten stuck in the chimney, how he had died, and why in the world he had been up on that house top. Had he been playing Santa Claus? Or had someone played a twisted joke and placed him there? I had so many questions.

"Okay." Starla stood and deposited her mug back on the counter. "Let's get going then. I want to see what this new life you have here in Nags Head is all about. I mean, I've heard about it through our conversations on the phone, but I want to see you in action."

"In action?" I questioned, mirroring her actions and returning my mug.

"Yeah, I want to see you solve this crime."

"I didn't say I would be solving this crime." I tried to sound convincing. Since I didn't, I leaned down and patted Java instead, avoiding Starla's gaze.

Everyone who knew me knew I lived for stuff like this. Outside of acting, crime fighting was my favorite sport—followed in second place by imitating Bob Ross.

"I can see that flame in your eyes. You've totally got the investigating bug in your system now. If you give up acting, at least you have this to fall back on."

Giving up acting . . . now that was a thought. I had to admit that sometimes I wondered if that might be the best option for me. Acting just kept on getting me in trouble. Then again, so did investigating.

We climbed into my Miata and took off toward the Curriers' house. I wondered if there would still be crime scene tape around it and if Jackson would be there.

Starla glanced out the window. "I just love everything about this beach town. Have I mentioned that yet?"

I smiled. I didn't mind her gushing, because I loved it too. It was partially the landscape—the sand dunes, the rolling waves, the beautiful sunsets. But it was mostly the people. The little community I'd found here was worth more to me than any amount of money.

As I pulled into the Curriers' neighborhood, my foot hit the brakes. The crime scene tape was still stretched around the house like a morbid Christmas decoration. But mostly what I saw was the familiar car.

Jackson's.

He stood on the front stoop, but his gaze was on me, almost like he'd anticipated me coming. I wondered if he had any more updates.

I hoped he did . . . and I hoped he would share.

CHAPTER
FOUR

I PLASTERED on a smile as Jackson walked toward my car.

I rolled down my window and utilized my most innocent expression as I said, "Good morning. If I'd known you were here, I would've brought you some coffee, honeybun."

Jackson's look clearly told me he saw right through me. He thought I was here to snoop. And maybe I was, but I also had a job to do.

"Joey." He nodded. "Starla. What brings you two here?"

"We thought the camera and production crew might be here," I said. "But, as I can see, they aren't. How are things going?"

"We're still investigating," he said. "I think we've collected most of the evidence here."

"Did you get any sleep last night?" I asked. Jackson still looked good, but he looked tired. The start of dark circles formed beneath his eyes, and even his motions seemed slower.

"Not much. I went home long enough to grab a shower, play with Ripley for a little while, and then I headed back here."

"You poor thing."

I put the car in park, and Starla and I climbed out. All the lights at the Curriers' house were off, but several cars still drove by, passengers gawking at the decorations. Last night's events seemed to taint the earlier excitement, replacing it with morbid curiosity.

I reached up and kissed Jackson's cheek, thankful that he didn't seem too aggravated by my presence. "Did you figure out how this Christian Nolan man died?"

The bigger question in my mind: was it murder?

"The initial report is that he suffocated while he was upside down in the chimney." Jackson's gaze drifted to the house. "It's called positional asphyxiation."

"So it *was* an accident?" I asked. "Nothing malicious?"

"To everyone's surprise, yes, it appears to have been an accident." Jackson stared at me, watching my expression and possibly looking for disappointment there.

"What about the man last night that the Ryderz driver saw?" I asked.

"He was gone. We're still looking for him, but right now we're assuming it was probably a joke or misunderstanding."

I wasn't so sure about that, but I kept my mouth shut.

"How in the world did that guy end up in that chimney?" Starla asked.

"I can't tell you how he ended up in the chimney," a new voice said. "But I might be able to add more to the story."

We looked over as Mr. Currier joined our conversation. He must've walked over from the neighbor's house. He had a mug of coffee in one hand, a newspaper under his arm, and he wore red and black pajamas with a matching robe. His house was now a crime scene, so he'd probably had to find somewhere else to stay.

"Mr. Currier," Jackson said. "I was about to call you."

"I saw the report on TV this morning." Mr. Currier frowned and took a long sip of his coffee, his face scrunching as if the liquid tasted bitter. "I recognized that man."

Jackson straightened, all his attention now on Mr. Currier. "Tell me more."

"About two days ago someone rang my doorbell." Mr. Currier shifted, his deepening frown pressing the corners of his lips. "It was this man trying to sell me a new security system for my home. I told him I wasn't interested, that I already had one."

"Go on," Jackson said.

"He asked me what kind of system I had." Mr. Currier shook his head, looking disgusted with himself. "I can't believe I was stupid enough to tell him. Looking back, it's obvious he was casing the joint and trying to figure out the best way to get into the house. He had me fooled. The man *looked* professional. He even wore a shirt from a security company."

"But this man was Nolan?" Jackson asked.

"It's definitely the same person."

Jackson squinted and looked off into the distance. "Interesting tactic. I'm going to need to talk to your neighbors and see if he came to their houses also."

"You think he was trying to get inside the house to rob us when he died?" Mr. Currier crossed his beefy arms as he waited for Jackson's response.

"That's what we're trying to figure out. Although I've never seen a case of someone trying to go down the chimney to enter a residence."

I stood back and observed, embracing the effort-less moment of nosiness. This moment was like a gift, kind of like those expensive grab bags actors got before awards ceremonies as companies tried to pimp out their products.

Mr. Currier let out a long breath. "I told him every door and window in my place had a sensor. If he really wanted to get into my house, the chimney was probably the only way. I practically handed him that information. I'm such an idiot. I haven't even told my wife that part yet."

"Is there anything inside your house of value?" Jackson asked.

"No. That's what really confuses me," Mr. Currier said. "My family and I . . . we don't have a lot. And what we do have . . . it's all Christmas doodads. That's where we put all of our extra money." He flung his hand back as if to display his house, which left no room for argument that his words were true.

I could see that these holiday novelties were really important to him.

"There are plenty of other neighborhoods in this town, neighborhoods where people have more money than we do here," he continued. "I'm not sure why we would be targeted."

"Thank you for this information." Jackson took a

step back. "If you think of anything else, please let us know."

"I will." Mr. Currier turned to Starla and I. "Do you know what the production plans are? The only good that can possibly come out of this is the money that will be given to charity on our behalf. I'm hoping we haven't been cut because of this."

Just as he asked the question, two SUVs pulled up. That had to be Thompson and the crew inside.

We were about to find out if we could move forward despite Christian Nolan's death or if he'd permanently decked the halls.

For the next hour, Mr. Currier, Jackson, and Thompson all stood outside trying to figure out when they could begin shooting again. I knew that we had a strict time schedule. The crew couldn't stay in town indefinitely, so the sooner they could film the house again, the better.

Finally, after some phone calls, it was decided that the show would be filmed again this evening. The police cleared the scene, the weather looked perfect, and the Curriers were on board. In fact, the Curriers were even allowed back inside their house.

As we stood outside discussing things, someone new entered our circle.

Fitz. He held a gift bag in his hands and shifted nervously. Just like yesterday, his gaze was completely and totally fixated on Starla. I had to smile. She had that effect on people. Well, on men, at least.

"I brought you something." He blushed, almost as if shy. But his gaze didn't appear timid. More like dopey teen infatuation.

If I had to guess, this guy had pictures of Starla hanging on his door and walls.

Starla took a step back. "That's so nice of you. But you didn't have to do this."

"Oh, but I wanted to." He grinned again.

I'd been in enough bad situations that I had a tendency to think in the worst-case scenarios. All I could imagine when Starla opened that bag was a snake popping out or some toxic powder flying in the air.

She reached into the bag, untangled some tissue paper, and revealed . . .

A salted caramel chocolate bar, a seashell Christmas ornament, and a beautiful snow globe.

Fitz shifted. "I heard that was your favorite candy bar. And I wanted you to have a Christmas ornament to remember your time here. And . . ."

Starla held the snow globe up to the light and watched as the glitter floated down around a miniature town inside the orb. It was an idyllic Christmas scene, and, when she twisted the knob on the bottom, "Silver Bells" began to play.

"And . . ." Fitz continued. "I know you and Joey are going to be riding in a snow globe for the parade, so I thought this would help you remember my house and this experience."

"This is just beautiful," Starla said. "But I couldn't possibly accept it."

"Nothing would make me happier than if you took this snow globe as yours."

Starla pulled the gift bag toward herself. "Well, every time I see these things, I'll think of you, Fitz. Thank you."

As sweet as her statement had sounded, I wasn't sure it was the best thing to say to someone like a Fitz, who obviously felt a bit of a puppy love toward her.

He held up a marker. "Also, if I could get that autograph that you had promised . . ."

"Of course," Starla said. "Where would you like me to sign?"

He held up a picture of her that appeared to be torn out of a magazine. "Right here would be perfect."

Starla handed me her gifts to hold while she signed her picture. Fitz beamed as she gave the paper back. "Here you go. And thanks so much again for the gifts."

Before she could say anything else, Thompson motioned to us. "We're going to need to go over a few things. While we have some extra time, I thought we could record some intros and maybe even some snippets for commercials. How does that sound?"

Everyone agreed.

I supposed that would keep me out of trouble. Otherwise, I'd end up trying to find out information that I had no business finding out. And that might put me on Santa's naughty list.

CHAPTER
FIVE

STARLA and I had just enough time to go back to my place to freshen up before filming. Just as we got there, a car from the airport pulled up with Starla's luggage. We waited by the steps, turning our backs to the cold wind as we waited for the driver.

He hurried around to the back of his car to grab her suitcases—all five of them—and started toward the front steps.

When the man spotted us, his eyes brightened with recognition. I supposed Starla and I should have been used to that, since our faces were relatively well known because of our film careers. But it still kind of amazed me.

I mean, I was a simple girl from the mountains of Virginia who thought she'd end up cutting hair for a living. Never had I ever envisioned strangers recognizing me in public or being interviewed on national TV shows or being stalked by the paparazzi.

The man smiled. He was fortysomething with a receding hairline, a short but powerful build, and defined muscles. He also had tattoos and a certain biker vibe to him.

"If it isn't Starla McKnight and Joey Darling. I didn't expect to see you two when I came here. Looks like it's my lucky day." He left the suitcases near our feet.

That didn't surprise me. When Starla flew, she used her real name, Amy Smith. It didn't have the same ring as her stage name. I had no room to talk. Joey Darling wasn't my real name either.

"I'm Dasher, by the way." The man paused and nodded.

"Like the reindeer?" I asked.

"Only at this time of year." He flashed a smile.

"Thank you so much for delivering my luggage." Starla reached into her wallet and handed him a twenty. "I really appreciate this. Now I can look pretty again."

I nearly rolled my eyes. Was my friend fishing for compliments? That was my guess. But I had to love her.

"To me, both of you will always be beautiful." The man paused for a moment as if he wasn't in a hurry. "Seeing you ladies just really made my day. I had no idea you two were in the area. If you don't mind me asking, what brings you out this way?"

"We're filming a Christmas special at one of the houses here," Starla said.

"Oh, the Curriers' place?" A strange emotion washed through his gaze. "I heard it was going to be featured on some TV show. I had no idea the two of you were going to be hosting it."

"We thought we'd do something a bit different and spread some Christmas cheer," I said.

He let out a grunt and nodded. "Hopefully everyone else will think of it that way also."

I paused. "What do you mean?"

He stared at me a moment before waving his hand in the air. "Oh, it's nothing."

"It sounds like something." I knew I shouldn't push, but I couldn't help myself.

"The thing is, I actually live in that neighborhood." He shrugged. "Some people don't love that their quiet has been disrupted like this. All the traffic can feel burdensome, you know what I mean?"

"Is there anybody in particular who doesn't like it?" I wasn't saying that person had anything to do with what was going on. As far as we knew, Christian Nolan had died in a freak accident. But questions never hurt anyone . . . until they did.

My gut told me there was more to the story.

"I'd have to say the Puddingtons have been very outspoken," Dasher said. "They've lived in the neighborhood for decades. Sometimes they act like they own it. They're early birds, and all the traffic and lights and Christmas music keep them up at night. I guess they have a point, yeah? I mean, the light display has disrupted everyone's lives. Most of us don't mind, though."

I stored their names in the back of my mind, just in case.

The man took a step back. "Anyway, it was great to meet both of you. Have a great day."

Starla turned toward me as he left. "Is everyone always so friendly around here?"

"Sometimes." *Unless they're killers.* I kept that thought to myself.

The majority of people I'd met were wonderful. Just because I had a few crimes that I solved under my belt didn't mean that danger lurked around every corner.

It didn't mean it didn't either.

We went inside and changed into the same clothes we'd worn last night. Right on time, our makeup gal stopped by to finish our looks and ensure we matched filming from last night. As we went through the process, my thoughts turned over what had happened.

So Christian Nolan had robbed a jewelry store. He'd served five years in prison. Three days ago, he'd been released. Two days ago, he'd shown up at the Curriers' house, pretending to be a security system salesman. One day ago, he turned up in the Curriers' chimney dead from positional asphyxiation.

As red gloss was brushed onto my lips, I tried to wrap my mind around why all of that may have happened. *Why* in the world someone would have thought it was a good idea to go down the chimney to get into a house? What was this man hoping to find inside? Did he think there was something of value that he could steal?

Or was that a smokescreen for something else? For that matter, maybe our original assumptions were wrong all together. Our Ryderz driver had said a man in the crowd had been watching and muttering something about wanting to make an impression.

I thought back to some of the interview notes we'd gone over before filming. I remembered the Curriers saying that they'd only moved into the house three years ago.

I wondered who lived in that house before. Did

that person have some type of connection to Christian Nolan?

Most likely, Jackson had already considered that angle. He was a great detective. But it was something I also wanted to look into myself.

But I shouldn't. And I *knew* I shouldn't. I needed to mind my own business. Why was that harder than trying not to peek at your presents when you knew where they'd been hidden?

Surprisingly, filming went off without a hitch. There were no dead bodies, no surprises, and nothing that set the crew on edge. Well, nothing except for what had already happened.

I had been looking over my shoulder the whole night, halfway expecting to see somebody doing something nefarious. There'd been nothing.

A good crowd had turned out to show community support. That was the way it was intended to be filmed. The whole show was about neighbors coming together and Christmas bringing a spirit of unity and forgiveness.

I stood in the middle of a field of plastic candy canes and took a second to clear my head.

Christmas music still rang out merrily through

the air. Right now, the featured song was "Frosty the Snowman." An inflatable Frosty danced with twirly motions in front of the house. Somehow, I could smell peppermint in the air, though I wasn't sure where the scent came from.

My gaze scanned the crowds. My friends, the Hot Chicks, had shown up this evening, as well as my buddies Zane and Phoebe. I'd already talked to all of them for a few minutes.

Now I was looking for someone else. Someone I most likely wouldn't recognize.

Was anybody here tonight familiar with Christian Nolan? Were they here to try to finish what he started? And, even more so, what *had* he tried to start?

What about the man that Ryderz driver had seen? Had he come back?

How about the Puddingtons? I wondered where exactly they lived. If they were nosy neighbors, had they seen anything?

I had so many questions—questions that were best kept to myself.

When the cameras shut off and things began to wrap up, Jackson wandered over. I stood in the middle of the sudsy snow display, near some life-sized reindeer. A smile played at the corner of his lips.

He leaned in close. "I know what you're thinking."

I looked up at him and batted my eyelashes innocently. He thought he knew me *sooo* well. Probably because he did.

"Whatsoever do you mean?" I asked with a sweet Southern accent.

"You're trying to figure out what happened. But I don't need to remind you that there was no crime here other than an unsuccessful break-in. The man was trying to break into the house, but he got stuck in the chimney. That's going to go in one of those articles about the dumbest criminals in the world."

I wished I could let it go at that. But my brain wouldn't stop. "How long did it take for you to catch this guy five years ago?"

"About a month. He hit four stores in the area, but he did a good job at eluding law enforcement."

"How much loot did he get away with?"

"About a half million dollars' worth of jewelry. And here's the thing. We never found it."

My eyes widened at that new factoid. "Are you serious? The jewelry is still out there somewhere?"

He looked into the distance, ever vigilant, before nodding. "That's correct. We checked with all of the pawn shops in this area and the surrounding areas.

We searched Nolan's apartment. It was nowhere to be found."

"So what do you think happened to it?" This story was getting more interesting all the time.

"I have no idea. Maybe he hid it. Since he's dead now, we might not ever know. It will be like Blackbeard's treasure."

My mind continued to race. "What if he left it here at this house? What if he was breaking in to get it?"

Jackson raised his eyebrows. "You really think he would've done that?"

"You're the detective. You tell me."

Jackson let out a deep chuckle. "Okay, smarty pants. I did have one of my guys check to see if Nolan had any connections with this house. It doesn't appear that he did."

"Ah ha! We're on the same wavelength, then."

"I've trained you well." He winked.

"Since there was no crime here, then this should be over, right? There shouldn't be any more danger?"

"By all appearances."

I nodded. But, in my life, nothing was this easy. Could it really be this time?

And was that a little bit of doubt I heard in Jackson's voice?

CHAPTER
SIX

THOUGH MOST OF the crew left the next morning, Starla and I were going to stay in town. One cameraman/associate producer was also sticking around to film snippets from the rest of my activities with Starla—mostly the charity dinner and parade.

I'd awoken at eight, taken a quick shower, and put on my favorite yoga pants and sweatshirt. I brewed some coffee and made myself comfortable in a plush chair—a twirly upholstered one near the patio doors with a perfect view of the ocean.

Just being here made me feel happy. Psychologists said that being at the beach was good for your health. I was inclined to agree.

The beach at Christmastime was even better. It was my first season here, but as I stared at the shore,

I saw someone had made a sandy snow family. Did it get any better than that?

Starla, in the meantime, was still sleeping. She'd never been much of a morning person. And that was okay because I was thankful for a few minutes alone.

I pulled my gaze away from the beach for long enough to look at the tree in the corner of the living room. I smiled at the sight of it. Jackson and I had put it up last week. We'd gone out and picked a Fraser fir. Jackson had hauled it upstairs, and we'd had fun decorating it together while listening to Christmas music.

Moments like those—simple moments—sometimes meant the most. I couldn't wait until Jackson and I were married and we could always do things like this together. I had visions of Easter egg hunts, carving pumpkins, and team building family activities—like solving mysteries together.

That was normal, right?

Halfway through my first cup of coffee, my phone rang. Jackson's name popped up on the screen. Already my day seemed brighter.

"Are you calling to tell me how brilliant I am?" I asked with a smile.

"You are pretty brilliant."

I sat up straighter. He now had my full attention. "I was just joking, but I'll take the flattery. But that's probably not what you called to tell me. What's going on?"

"Since it's public information, I thought I'd let you know that someone tried to break into the Curriers' house last night."

My pulse raced at his words. "What do you mean?"

"We got a call about three in the morning. The Curriers' alarm went off. Whoever tried to break in this time obviously didn't do the same research that Christian Nolan did. He tried to get in through a window."

I set my coffee down on an end table beside me. "And the alarm went off?"

"It did, but not before the guy got inside and wandered around for a bit."

That had been brazen. "What happened?"

"This guy was still in the dining room when Mr. Currier came downstairs holding a baseball bat. As soon as the man saw him, he darted out the window."

"So Mr. Currier didn't get a good look at him?"

"No, he was wearing black from head to toe. There was nothing to see."

I leaned back in my seat and processed that information. "Very interesting. Did you dig any deeper to see if there was any connection with this house and Christian Nolan?"

"We did," Jackson said. "At first, we didn't see any obvious connections to him and this place. But, as it turns out, an old high school friend used to live there. His family moved four years ago."

My heart quickened. Was that the lead the police needed to get some answers? It seemed like it to me. "So, this guy and his family owned it during the time when Nolan was robbing the jewelry stores?"

"Correct."

"Did the family, by chance, sell the house fully furnished?" It wasn't uncommon for people in this area to have second homes. When they sold those homes, they usually came with everything included —all the way down to sheets, towels, and sometimes even old toilet paper.

"As a matter of fact, the home was sold with all of the furniture and decorations inside."

I held up a mental V for Victory. I didn't know why finding answers was so incredibly satisfying, but it was. Almost like watching cooking videos or popping bubble wrap.

"In fact, this family had pack-rat tendencies. I guess the Curriers had a lot to sort through before they moved in."

"Are you thinking what I'm thinking?"

"That depends." Humor deepened his voice. "What are you thinking?"

"I think Christian Nolan must've hidden his stolen loot there. It was probably all he could think about while he was in prison. As soon as he got out, he knew he had to retrieve it in order to make a new life for himself."

"I'd say you're pretty smart, Joey Darling."

"Why, thank you. But if Nolan is dead, who broke in? That's the question."

"Maybe he told someone else that the jewelry was there. We're trying to track down some leads."

That would be an interesting twist. "Good luck with it."

"Thanks. I think we're going to need it."

"Oh, and the man who delivered Starla's luggage said something about a disagreement the Curriers had with a neighbor. Apparently, not everyone likes the traffic and noise."

"I'll see what I can find out."

As I ended the call, my mind raced with possibilities. However, none of them were about the holiday celebrations planned for this week. No, all I could think about was Christmas . . . and crime.

A few minutes later, Starla emerged from her downstairs bedroom donning an all-pink pajama set —from her flannel bottoms all the way to her silky bathrobe.

"Good morning, girlfriend," she called, seeming especially perky.

"Good morning."

"Please tell me you have stuff to make avocado toast? It's all I've been thinking about since I woke up this morning."

I stood and walked into the kitchen. "As a matter of fact, I do."

"You're the best." She plopped down in one of the wooden chairs at the kitchen table.

I poured her some coffee, added copious amounts of cream and sugar, and set it in front of her.

"I wish I had someone to do this for me every day," she mumbled. "Thank you."

I totally understood the sentiment. My friend liked to be pampered. Sometimes, so did I. But I never expected it.

As I got to work on breakfast, I glanced at my friend. She'd picked up her phone and was furiously typing something.

"Everything okay?" I asked.

Starla glanced up and frowned apologetically. "Sorry. I'm just catching up on some social media.

My followers are just begging me to post. At least, that's what my social media site is telling me. *Fans of Starla McKnight haven't heard from her in twenty-four hours.* What will they do?" Her voice rose dramatically, and her lips formed a perfect "O."

I had to laugh. Sometimes I thought Starla and I were cut from the same cloth. It was nice to be around somebody who understood the perils and pressures of fame and Hollywood.

However, the fishing for compliments? Being concerned what others were thinking? Constantly looking for validation?

I didn't miss any of that. Seeing her now reminded me so much of my old life.

"By the way, I got an email from David." She lowered her phone, and her frown deepened.

David Melton was Starla's ex-boyfriend. The two had dated for four months before breaking up three weeks ago. He was a former pro baseball player, and their publicists had introduced them so they could both get good press. Starla had seemed so happy at the start of their relationship.

But things had gone south. David had lost his baseball contract, and he'd changed into a different person, apparently.

I straightened. "You said you guys broke up. So why is he still emailing?"

"We did." Starla raised her eyebrows, looking skeptical. "But he desperately wants to get back together. He said he wants to fly out and meet me so we can talk."

That was generous of him, I supposed. "All the way across the country?"

"He doesn't know exactly where I am. He said it didn't matter how far away I might be, though. He just wanted to see me."

"What are you going to tell him?"

"I told him I'm not interested in getting back together with him. I told him I had a new boyfriend. Named Fitz." She flashed a mischievous smile.

"Are you serious?"

"No, I didn't say that." She rolled her eyes. "But I did think about it. I just want him to leave me alone. He is the one who acted all jerky and had all these problems with committing. Now he's changed his mind and he expects me to also? I don't think so."

"Hopefully he will take no for an answer."

"Exactly." She took another sip of her coffee. "So, was that Jackson you were talking to?"

"It sure was." I told her about the new developments on the case as I sliced into the avocado.

Starla's mouth dropped open. "Someone actually tried to break into the house? That's kind of scary."

"I know, isn't it? It makes me wonder what exactly is going on."

"There's something valuable inside that house. I don't care what Mr. Currier says."

I was inclined to agree.

I topped our toast with a drizzle of olive oil, some red pepper flakes, and fennel. My mouth was already watering, and I couldn't wait to dig in.

"Breakfast is served," I said, presenting my creation with a flourish. "Let's eat and talk about the rest of our day."

We needed to make a list and check it twice.

CHAPTER
SEVEN

STARLA and I did a few interviews for local TV stations, trying to drum up publicity for *Lit*. They had been mostly painless.

Of course, my mind kept drifting back toward those legs I'd seen coming out of the chimney. I wondered what Jackson was doing and if the police had discovered anything new.

When he called and asked me if I wanted to meet for coffee, I was thrilled. Starla wanted to take a quick nap, so it worked out well. I could use some time with Jackson.

I met him at Sunrise, where I ordered my favorite latte, gave Java a pat on the head, and then sat down.

Jackson leaned across the table and kissed my cheek. "It's good to see you."

"It's always good to see you too. I know you're busy."

"Yes, unfortunately, I don't have a lot of time," Jackson said. "But I always have time for you. Are you hanging in there?"

I nodded, feeling myself melt a little bit at his warmth and concern. "Yes, I'm doing fine. *Lit* is pretty awesome, isn't it? I told you it would be."

"I do like the concept. Christmas, charity, community . . . what else do you need?"

"Exactly." I took a sip of my coffee. "My dad used to always take me driving around the neighborhoods near our house so we could look at Christmas lights. Those are some of my favorite memories."

He offered a soft smile. "I'm sure they are." He shifted. "Listen, I know I shouldn't tell you this, but it will be public soon enough."

My pulse raced. "What is it?"

"We just heard back from the coroner. He discovered some bruising on Christian Nolan that's calling into question whether or not this was an accident."

"How could this be anything but an accident?" I tried to visualize it being something different. My gut told me there was more to this story, but common sense wasn't always my strength.

"We believe someone may have knocked him out and then put him in the chimney."

I sucked in a quick breath. "I guess the bruising matches that?"

"It does. Plus, there's a contusion on the back of his head."

"That's horrible."

"I know. That said, this means there could be a killer out there. You need to be extra careful."

"You think the person who did this is the same one who broke into the Curriers'?"

He lowered his voice. "Actually, the family realized there was something missing from the house."

I sucked in a breath. "Something was actually stolen? I thought they didn't have anything of value."

"They didn't think they did. But apparently, they had some Depression era glass in their china cabinet. It used to be their parents', and they never really thought anything of it. When Tammy went to check something, she realized some pieces were missing."

"How much is the stuff worth?"

"They had some purple colored glass, which, from what I understand, is the most sought after. Still, it was all probably worth less than a thousand." He shrugged. "But I've seen people break in for less."

I shook my head, trying to wrap my mind around how all these events connected. "The plot thickens, huh?"

"I guess you could say that."

I shifted in my seat, still playing with my coffee mug as my thoughts raced. "Jackson, did you check with Nolan's former friend? Wouldn't he be the most obvious suspect here?"

Jackson released a long breath. "I can see where you'd think that. I actually looked into his whereabouts because I wanted to ask him a few questions."

"And?" I held my breath, waiting to hear what he'd found out.

"And he died two years ago in a car accident."

I frowned. That sounded tragic . . . and, less importantly, like a shriveled-up lead.

"Was it the killer who broke into the Curriers' house last night?" I asked, still trying to make sense of it all.

"We don't know. There's a chance it was someone else who saw an opportunity. Hard to say at this point."

I could tell he was about to wrap up, but I still had more questions. I grabbed his hand before he could leave. "Who would want to kill Christian Nolan?"

"The most obvious answer? One of the jewelry store owners he ripped off." Jackson glanced at his watch. "I'm going to question them now."

"Be safe, Jackson," I said. "I hope you find some

answers so you can get back to being my security detail."

"I will. You too."

I headed back to my place and picked up Starla. I gave her a quick update.

"I can't believe that." Starla's eyes widened as she took another sip of her coffee.

"I can't either. It's all so crazy."

An idea began bobbing in my head, a good sign whenever I was fishing for answers. "Do you mind if we make one quick stop?"

Starla shrugged. "Why not? I don't have anything else to do."

I poked around on my phone for a minute until I found the information I needed. Then Starla and I were off, driving toward the Curriers. However, they weren't the ones I wanted to talk to.

Instead, I pulled up to a house four down from the Christmas display.

"Where are we?" Starla asked, glancing around in confusion.

"I'm trying to find out some information. But I'm going to need a cover story. Follow my lead."

She shrugged. "Whatever you say."

I straightened my evergreen-colored tunic, trying to make myself presentable as I walked to the door. I rang the bell and waited.

Finally, an older woman, probably in her seventies, answered. She stared at me a moment before her eyes lit with recognition. "You two are those actresses who are here in town, aren't you?"

She opened the door wider, revealing an adorable red Christmas vest and a light up holiday necklace. She didn't exactly look like the Scrooge she'd been described as.

"We are. We were filming just down the street. We just wanted to take the time to meet some neighbors. Part of our reason for being here is to get to know the community better."

"Then please, by all means, come in, come in." She ushered us inside. "My husband just ran to the store for some milk. I made some cookies. Would you like some?"

The heavenly aroma of snickerdoodles filled the air and made my stomach grumble, even though I wasn't hungry. Despite that realization, when she offered me some, I accepted, along with some hot chocolate.

My waistline was not going to agree with this. Maybe I'd drink smoothies all day tomorrow to make up for it.

Once we were settled in the living room with our treats and had done a sufficient amount of chitchat, I turned back to Mrs. Puddington, ready to get down to business.

"There's been a lot of excitement in the neighborhood, huh?" I started.

"There sure has. More than I like. But it is nice to see everyone coming together."

Hmm . . . this wasn't exactly the story Dasher had told me.

"I'm sure the traffic can be frustrating," I said, still fishing. Jackson had taught me that fishing required lots and lots of patience.

"It can be. At first, my husband and I were frustrated. Then we realized we didn't want to be Scrooges, and we lightened up. Anything that makes the community come together isn't something we should complain about."

"That's true . . ." There went that lead.

I did have one other thing I wanted to ask her about, though.

"Did you know the family who lived there before the Curriers moved in?" I continued, taking a sip of my hot chocolate.

"Oh, yes, we did. The Manicottis. Sweetest family."

"They had a son, correct?"

"That's right. BJ. He was a good boy. He cut my grass for me, and even helped install our mailbox when someone ran it over once."

That surprised me. "Did I hear that the man found in the chimney had been friends with him at one time?"

I had to be careful—I knew I was pushing it.

"You mean Christian?" Mrs. Puddington shook her head, a far-off look in her eyes. "He seemed like a nice boy who'd been dealt a bad hand in life. It's such a shame about what happened. Such a shame."

Coming here I'd confirmed one thing: the Puddingtons were not responsible for this crime. Not by a long shot.

CHAPTER
EIGHT

THAT NIGHT, I lay in bed, reflecting on everything that had happened today.

Jackson had told me that none of the jewelry store owners had panned out as suspects. Two had moved from the area, one had retired and was in a wheelchair, and the fourth had an alibi for the night of the murder.

The Puddingtons obviously weren't responsible. We were just scratching the surface here, but I couldn't help but wonder who else might be guilty.

Not that it was any of my business. But that had never stopped me before.

I began counting imaginary reindeer instead of sheep and trying to turn my brain off for long enough to fall asleep. A sound downstairs caused me to sit up in bed with a start.

A cold sweat spread across my forehead. I'd had enough bad things happen to me for my radar to instantly go on alert when trouble was near. Children had their Santa tracker. I had my mental danger tracker.

It made sense in my world.

Starla was in the house, I reminded myself. She could just be wandering around or going to the bathroom. I had a feeling that wasn't the case, though.

I reached under my bed and grabbed my baseball bat. I always kept one there, just in case. I rose to my feet and crouched as I walked to the door.

I paused a moment. What was I doing? Did I really think I could take on an intruder with a baseball bat? Had my past experiences taught me nothing?

I reached for my phone and quickly dialed Jackson's number instead.

He answered on the first ring, his voice instantly alert and concerned. "Joey, are you okay? What's going on?"

We'd been through this a few times before.

"I think somebody might be inside my house," I whispered. "Somebody besides Starla."

"Stay where you are. I'll be right there."

Just as I ended the call, a scream echoed down the hallway. As much as I wanted to honor my promise to Jackson, I could not stay here. Not if my friend could be in danger.

I burst into the hallway and raced down the stairs toward Starla's room. As I did, I gripped the bat in my hand and prayed I didn't have to use it. Maybe Starla had simply seen a spider and freaked out.

But deep down inside, I knew that probably wasn't the case. Something had happened.

I hesitated only a second as my hand gripped Starla's door handle. Then I barged inside, my adrenaline pumping. I couldn't afford to waste any time—not if my friend's life could be on the line.

I scanned the dark space around me, halfway expecting to see a shadowy figure lurking. Instead, I spotted Starla on the floor holding her head and looking confused.

I hit the switch behind me and light filled the room. I took one more glance around to make sure no one was hiding, then rushed toward my friend and dropped down beside her.

"Oh my goodness," I said quickly. "Are you okay? What happened?"

I knelt beside Starla and examined her for any sign of injuries. From what I could tell, she was okay, just shaken. Her hair was tousled, her eyes wide, and her skin pale. But there were no cuts or blood.

Thank goodness.

"I don't know what happened." Starla's voice trembled as she raked her hand through her hair. "I woke up and this man wearing a black mask was standing over my bed. He said, 'Where is it?' I said, 'Where is what?' Before we could continue our *conversation*, something banged on the window."

A banging on the window? I hadn't expected to hear that. "And then?"

"The man got spooked. He threw me on the floor, and I hit my head. I must've blacked out for a minute, but when I came to again, he was gone."

Unease sloshed in my gut. "Jackson is on his way right now. But are you sure you heard someone banging on the window outside?"

"Yes, I am sure. Somebody was out there, and whoever it was, the noise scared this man away." She let out a restrained cry. "Oh, Joey. I thought for a minute that he was going to kill me."

I swallowed hard. I did not like the sound of this. Not one bit.

Just then, I heard another noise up on the housetop.

No, make that on my deck.

Footsteps.

And then a knock at my door.

"Joey, it's me. Jackson."

I rushed to let him inside.

"Do you have any idea what this man was talking about when he asked 'where is it?'" Jackson asked Starla.

We'd moved upstairs into my kitchen and sat around the table. Since we were already up, I decided to go ahead and brew my favorite coffee roast. The pot gurgled and burped on the counter as Starla ran through what had happened.

Starla stared into the distance, still looking slightly dazed. "I have no idea what he could be referring to. I only brought five suitcases with me, and they're filled almost completely with clothes, makeup, and hair products. I mean, I do have my computer and my cell phone, but I can't imagine that someone would break in to get those things. I have a couple necklaces and rings."

Just then, Jackson's gaze fixated out the window, and he stood. His muscles went rigid.

That was when I knew something was wrong.

"What is it?" I held my breath, wondering what it would be now. Trouble kept coming like it was Santa doing rounds to houses on Christmas morning.

"Someone is outside." He stepped near the wall and shooed Starla and I out of sight.

A shiver rushed down my spine. Had the bad guy

stuck around, waiting for Jackson to leave again? Just what was this guy planning?

"Stay here," Jackson muttered.

The next thing I knew, Jackson took off toward the door. He was going after this guy.

I closed my eyes and prayed for his safety. I knew I'd have to get used to this when I got married to a cop, but it was never fun seeing the people you loved in danger. And that seemed to be the story of my life.

CHAPTER
NINE

TO MY HORROR, Starla pulled out her phone and began filming everything.

"What are you doing?" I nearly screeched.

"This will be great for my social media feed."

I wanted to argue, to fuss. But there was a time I might have done the same thing.

Before I could devise anything to say that wouldn't make me seem like a total hypocrite, Jackson came back inside with somebody in tow.

My eyes widened when I saw Fitz Currier there. The man looked flushed, nervous, and excited. His cheeks were red, his breathing was heavy, but he had a dopey smile on his face as he waved at Starla.

"Is this the person who broke into the house?" Starla stood against the kitchen counter, her sweatshirt pulled close and a horrified look on her face.

Her phone was now lowered and her video seemingly forgotten.

Jackson kept a tight grip on Fitz, not letting go, as they stood in front of us. Sand was plastered to Fitz's face, leading me to assume that Jackson had tackled him on the beach.

He was such a tough guy. I loved it.

"I can't believe I'm in Joey Darling's house." Fitz looked around, as if soaking everything in and relishing the moment.

I shook my head, trying not to feel flabbergasted. Was that really all he was thinking about at this very moment? It seemed weird and inappropriate.

"Fitz, did you go inside this house earlier?" Jackson still had a hand on the man as if he feared he might take off in a run—or something worse, like lunging toward me or Starla.

"No, I didn't come inside the house," Fitz said, his gaze starry eyed still on Starla.

"Then what were you doing outside staring up at us?" Jackson continued. "I saw you out there."

"I came here because I was curious. I know I probably shouldn't have, but I wanted to see where Starla and Joey were staying. I've had a mad crush on both of them for a long time, but mostly Starla." He gazed at her longingly again.

"So you just happened to be here when somebody

broke into the house?" Jackson's dry, no-nonsense voice made it clear he was skeptical.

"As a matter of fact, yes," Fitz said. "I was standing outside when I saw someone break into the house through one of the windows. I feared that something bad might be happening."

"So you called the police?" Jackson filled in.

"No." Fitz frowned and guilt flashed in his eyes. "I knew I didn't have time for that. Instead, I walked to the windows and tried to figure out what this guy was doing. When I saw him attacking Starla, I knew I had to take action. I banged on the window to scare him away. And it worked."

"Just to clarify, you're saying that you did *not* break into Joey's house?" Jackson said.

"That's correct. This is the first time I have ever been inside of this house. And I couldn't be happier. I mean, mostly I'm happy because you ladies are okay. But now that I know that, I'm absolutely thrilled to be here."

Jackson's gaze met mine, and I could tell he thought this guy was a loon. Next, Jackson's gaze turned to Starla. "Does he look like the guy who was in your bedroom?"

Starla looked Fitz up and down. "The man in my bedroom was wearing all black, including a mask. And I'm pretty sure he was taller and beefier."

"So you don't think this was the guy?" Jackson clarified.

"I'm pretty sure it wasn't Fitz, unless he changed clothes between now and then."

"I didn't," Fitz rushed. "Do you really think I would've worn a white T-shirt if I had planned on breaking in?"

"I've seen dumber criminals do dumber things," Jackson said.

"I don't think it was him, Jackson," Starla said.

The next instance, Starla rose to her feet and pulled Fitz into a hug. "You may have saved my life tonight," she told him. "Thank you so much for stalking me."

Jackson took Fitz to the station to get his official statement. He also sent out an officer to search for fingerprints and other evidence, but he warned us to temper our expectations. Most likely, there wouldn't be a lot found.

Starla and I had stayed awake for the rest of the night chatting with each other and catching up. We both knew there was no way we were going to sleep after what had happened. I tried to talk to her about why she'd filmed what happened earlier, but she didn't seem interested.

My gut told me something else was going on with Starla. I just wasn't sure what. She seemed more insecure than usual.

To my surprise, Jackson had shown up bright and early in the morning with a fresh round of coffee from Sunrise.

"Can I come in?" he asked.

"Please do." I took my coffee and walked with Jackson to the kitchen table.

It was a beautiful morning to watch the sunrise from inside. The colors were a reddish-pink, and they boldly smeared across the sky, announcing the arrival of a brand-new day.

Such a beautiful start to the day seemed to promise good things—and I hoped that promise was true.

"I came to give you both an update." Jackson paused and leaned against the wall, crossing his arms over his chest. "We took Fitz's statement, just like I said we would. But, in the process, we also discovered a few interesting things."

"Like what?" Starla took a sip of her drink and nodded with approval.

"We decided to look at his computer records." Jackson's eyes danced.

I'd seen that look before. He usually got it when he discovered a lead. So what had he discovered now?

"And . . .?" I asked.

"It turns out that Fitz has been in contact with Christian Nolan."

My eyes widened. "He was in contact with the dead man? No way . . ."

"I didn't want to believe it myself, but it's true."

"Why in the world would he be in contact with Nolan?" Starla asked.

I tried to think it through and come up with possible reasons, but I came up blank.

"It turns out that when Fitz realized Nolan had a connection with the house his family had bought, he got curious. He started corresponding with Nolan, and they had somewhat of a pen pal relationship."

"That's weird." I took a sip of my drink and let that revelation sink in.

Jackson nodded. "I think so too. But Fitz is a little different. In fact, we discovered he has a fascination with all things crime-related."

"That's weird?" I asked, thinking about myself and my own obsessions. It seemed perfectly normal.

Jackson gave me a look. "Yeah, it kind of is. Not only does he like crime dramas and watch them religiously, he also wrote research papers in high school on serial killers. His mom said it was just a silly phase he was going through. Who knows what the truth is?"

"Does this have anything to do with Nolan's death?" Starla asked.

"That's what we're trying to figure out. Based on the emails and texts that we've read so far, we haven't been able to find anything to tie him to it. That's not to say he isn't guilty in some way."

Starla lowered herself into a chair, her hands still gripping her coffee. "So is Fitz in custody now?"

"We are still holding him down at the station. There's only one problem with our theory. Fitz is deathly afraid of heights. We've had several people attest to that."

"For that reason, you don't think he could have killed Christian?" I didn't want to make any assumptions.

"That's how it looks—although people have been known to overcome their fears in the heat of the moment before committing crimes. We're not ruling him out as a suspect. I just thought the two of you would like to know."

"Yes, we definitely wanted to know," I said. "Thank you for coming by. And thank you for the coffee."

He straightened and rolled his shoulders back. "What are you two up to today?"

"We're meeting with the mayor. And running through everything for the parade tomorrow. Tonight is the charity dinner down at the school. You're coming, right?"

"I don't know—I thought my role acting as security detail was over."

"I always want you to be my security detail."

He grinned and winked at me. "If you need anything else, give me a ring. I'll be working today, but I'm only a call away if you need me."

I stood and walked him to the door, my hand reaching for his. "Thank you for everything, Jackson. As always, I don't know what I would do without you."

We paused at the door, and Jackson leaned toward me. His lips briefly brushed mine. "And I don't know what I would do without you keeping me busy solving crimes."

A smile stretched across his lips.

CHAPTER
TEN

STARLA and I sat down in my living room to paint our nails. As we did, we popped on the TV to watch some news.

"You know what I would like to see?" Starla asked, shaking up a bottle of Kelly green polish. "I want to see you and Jackson get your own reality TV show."

I nearly snorted. "Me and Jackson? He would never get on board with something like that."

"Why not? He has the looks for it."

"But he's a no drama kind of guy. The last thing he wants is fame or stardom." I plucked a candy apple red bottle from my collection and opened it.

"He must not mind it entirely, because he is marrying you. Fame kinda comes with the territory."

Carefully, I painted my first nail. "I suppose, but

Jackson just isn't the type to relish in it. A reality show would be fun though, wouldn't it? Or the worst idea ever."

"You two would be very entertaining."

Our gazes went to the TV as a news story came on. My eyes widened when I heard my name and Starla's. The news footage cut to the scene at the Curriers' house on the first day of filming, and a voiceover told viewers about the catastrophe that had happened there two days ago.

Starla paused with her polish brush in the air. "Did you see that one shot they took of me? I looked awful."

The camera crew had caught some footage of Starla and me talking with the police after the dead body had been found. Starla's face had looked lax with surprise. Her lips had been parted, her eyes wide, and her shoulders tense. I didn't think she looked horrible, but my friend was super image conscious.

I painted another nail, more slowly this time. "I wonder if this is the first time they've run the story?"

"Why would it matter?" Starla asked.

I sat up straighter and pointed to the TV. "This looks like an interview the Curriers did before we came. Look behind them."

"It's the dining room. Okay . . ."

"There's a china cabinet, and it has all that Depression era glassware—the purple stuff that was stolen."

She sucked in a breath. "That could be how someone discovered they even had that in their home."

"Exactly. This guy who broke in could have seen this interview, known the valuable glassware was in the house, and broken in to steal it." Excitement raced through me.

"Are you going to call Jackson?" Starla asked.

"It would be irresponsible not to, right?"

"See? I told you. You have this detective thing down to an art." She capped her polish and began blowing on her nails.

I shrugged, even though Starla's words secretly thrilled me. "I don't know about that."

I painted my last nail, put my supplies back into a basket, and then slipped away to call Jackson. He thanked me for the update.

When I returned to the living room, I saw Starla staring at her phone with a scowl on her face. "You have got to be kidding me."

"What's going on?" Another surprise? And, when I said surprise, I meant headache. Setback. Tragedy. I lowered myself into the chair across from her and waited to hear what had happened.

She rolled her eyes and let out a sigh. "I just got an email from one of my buddies back in LA. She heard David is headed out this way to pay me a visit."

"Did you tell him where you were?"

"No . . ." She chuckled, like it was a dumb question. "But there was a news story on TV about this whole fiasco. I'm sure he could have figured it out."

I frowned. "That makes sense. But why would he come all the way out here to see you, especially after you told him not to?"

"Because he desperately wants to talk face to face." Starla rolled her eyes again as her voice turned mocking.

I ignored her childish behavior as a thought hit me so hard I nearly bit my tongue. "You don't think that man last night could've been David, do you?"

Starla shrugged, like she'd already thought about it. "The height and build *do* match."

"But why would David break in and ask you where 'it' was?" What sense did that make? I leaned back, trying to piece it together.

My friend frowned and held up a hand to examine her nails. "Maybe it's because he has been asking for a ring back that he gave me. It's supposedly worth thousands. I told him no, that it had been a gift."

"What . . . he gave you a ring?" Why hadn't I heard about this yet? It seemed like something my friend might mention to me.

Sharla shrugged and blew on her nails. "It wasn't that big of a deal. It was more for show than anything. Our entire relationship was practically scripted just to get tabloid attention and keep us in the public eye."

I shook my head, unable to imagine my friend going that far just to help her career. But, right now, I had to concentrate on the issues at hand. "So you think David would've broken in just trying to get that ring back?"

Starla's gaze met mine. "I think it's a very good possibility."

———

Jackson picked us up an hour later so we could go down to the mayor's office and run through things for the parade tomorrow. As he drove us, we gave him the update on David. Starla pulled up his picture, took a screenshot, and sent it to Jackson so he could have it on hand.

"So you really think your ex could be behind the break-in last night?" Jackson glanced at her in his rearview mirror.

"I wouldn't put it past him." Starla's voice dripped with bitterness. "Our breakup was ugly, and he didn't take it well. Who knows when he got here?"

At her words, a thought hit me. "Jackson, the man that Ryderz driver saw on the first night of filming . . . he was tall with dark hair and a beard, right?"

"Correct."

"That fits David's description."

Starla gasped. "You don't think . . . "

"I'm not saying he had anything to do with Nolan's death. I'm just saying . . ." What was I saying? "What if it was David who was there?"

"We'll keep our eyes open for him," Jackson said. "I'll see what I can find out."

I leaned back in my seat, not liking where my thoughts were going. "How about Fitz? What's going on with him? Any updates you are allowed to share?"

"We're still holding him right now, but he hasn't owned up to anything. Right now, he remains our best suspect in the death of Christian Nolan. What we are unsure about is why."

"It seems like Fitz might have an obsessive personality," I suggested. "What if he became obsessed with Nolan, lured him to the house, and then they had a fight of some sort?"

"I suppose that could be a possibility," Jackson said. "But, until we have proof, there's not much we can do. We just have to keep searching for the truth."

"See?" Starla said with a teasing tone in her voice. "The two of you would be perfect on some type of reality TV show. I am telling you, it would be ratings gold."

Jackson and I exchanged a look. I tried to read his expression, and it was just as I thought it would be. He thought the idea was ridiculous.

He had too much common sense for the whole Hollywood scene. I wasn't complaining. Jackson was my dream guy, and I was going to hold onto him forever.

And I didn't mean that in a creepy way.

We arrived at the mayor's office where a woman named Annabelle met with us. She was in her late twenties. She wore a red dress and her cheeks were rosy, matching her smile. She was going to be our main contact for the event.

"This is going to be our best Christmas parade yet," Annabelle said. "We've had great attendance over the past few years as more and more people have been staying in town for Christmas."

"I guess that's good for business, right?" I shifted in the tiny space called her office, feeling a bit claustrophobic. The woman had three Christmas trees set up, a wreath on her door, and colorful lights strung everywhere.

"It sure is. Anyway, this Christmas parade just helps us to feel that Christmas spirit in town even more. We have more than thirty floats that will be participating. Since you two are our grand marshals, you'll lead the procession."

"Awesome," I said, trying to keep the conversation short so I could leave this room.

"The mayor wants me to go over the parade route with you, just so you can be aware of everything that's going on. I also know that security will need to be stepped up because of the two of you being involved." She nodded at Jackson. "We're working with the police department so we can make sure everyone is safe and that the parade is an enjoyable time for all."

"That's what I like to hear," I told her. "Safety first."

"We're actually going to be starting the parade down at the school," she said. "There's a craft show and farmers market there today. I realize that people might recognize you and come up to you. I hope that's not a problem."

"We're used to it," Starla said. "It shouldn't be a problem."

As she said the words, I remembered everything

that was going on and wondered if it was wise. However, Jackson would be with us, so we should be fine. If we wouldn't be, I had no doubt that Jackson would speak up.

On the drive there, Annabelle yammered on and on about details concerning the parade. I tried to pay attention. I really did. But as "Winter Wonderland" played on the radio, I mentally found myself singing along and envisioning the song playing out.

I really did love this time of the year. It was my favorite.

Before I realized how much time had passed, we pulled up to the school and parked. We climbed out, Annabelle hugging her clipboard and looking all business. She pointed at several areas we needed to know about, and I tried my best to pay attention.

Starla nudged me. I stiffened and followed her gaze.

The blood left my face when I saw a familiar face there.

David. Starla's ex.

He was here at the art show.

And he was staring right at us.

CHAPTER
ELEVEN

"JACKSON!" I yelled.

He jerked his head toward me, his body instantly going into fight mode.

"It's David," I said. "Starla's ex."

I pointed to the man in the distance. As I did, Jackson stepped toward him. David took off in a run.

That was never a good sign. In fact, it usually indicated guilt. *Guilty is as guilty does.* I wasn't sure if that was a saying or not, but it should be.

I clutched Starla's arm as we watched Jackson chase David through the crowds.

"I can't believe this," Starla said. "What was David doing here, and why did he run instead of talking to us?"

I kept quiet about my theory—the theory that he could be mixed up in the events from this week.

Annabelle joined us, looking both perplexed and horrified.

"It sure is an exciting day here in Nags Head. I can assure you, it's not always this crazy." She let out a quick, brittle laugh.

Part of me wanted to argue with her. I had been in the middle of more than my fair share of crimes since coming here. However, some of them had occurred because trouble had found me. Other times, I had to admit that crime had followed me.

Annabelle lowered her voice. "By the way, I heard what happened when you were filming."

"I suppose everyone has at this point." News traveled fast in small towns.

"My little sister goes to high school with Fitz. I heard that Mr. Currier has quite the temper."

"Does he?" I questioned. Was she implying that the father might be guilty?

I chewed on that thought for a moment, but I couldn't see it. Still, I stored the information away in the back of my mind.

Right now, my bets were on David. He'd obviously come here searching for Starla.

But why? Was he really going to these great lengths to try to get that ring back? It screamed of desperation to me. But desperate people did desperate things, so I wouldn't put anything past him.

A few minutes later, Jackson appeared, hauling David behind him. His expression looked stormy and his demeanor rigid and insubordinate.

"David." Starla stared at him coolly and gave him a slight head nod.

David looked just like I remembered him. He was tall with dark hair and a beard. But his gaze didn't look stable right now. Instead, his eyes looked shifty and almost desperate.

Jackson led him back toward his police SUV and away from the crowd to talk. Starla, Annabelle, and I followed, but I wasn't sure if we were welcome or not. I'd stay until Jackson shooed me away.

"Do you want to tell me what you're doing here in town?" Jackson pushed him against the SUV and hulked in front of him.

Annabelle slipped away. I didn't ask her where she was going or what she was doing. All of my attention was on this conversation. I didn't like it when people threatened me or my friends, so I hoped we were able to find answers.

"I've missed you, Starla." David's gaze drifted to my friend. "I knew when I heard you were here that this was my chance to talk to you again."

"I've already said everything I needed to say to you on the phone and through text messages."

"I just want another chance."

"You've already had multiple chances, and you blew them all," Starla said. "No more chances. Does it look like I have 'sucker' tattooed across my forehead?"

"I know I had a few instances of using poor judgment—"

"Poor judgment?" Starla let out a dry laugh. "If you call cheating on me poor judgment, then so be it. But I am not putting myself through that again."

"I've turned over a new leaf," David insisted.

Starla rolled her eyes. "I've heard that before."

Jackson turned toward David. "When did you get into town?"

He shrugged, totally on the defensive and full of attitude. "Last night around six."

"And where did you go after you arrived?" Jackson asked.

"Why?" David suddenly tensed as if realizing this could be a trick question.

"Just answer the question," Jackson said. "Where did you go?"

"I went down to Willie Wahoos. Why is that relevant? This isn't a police matter. It's between me and my girl."

"I'm not your girl," Starla shot.

Jackson pressed his lips together, looking like his patience was being tested. "Because someone broke into their house last night and threatened Starla. Would you happen to know anything about that, David?"

David's face lost all of its color. "Whoa, whoa, whoa. I have no idea what you're talking about. I've done a lot of dumb things in my life, but I've never broken into someone's home. Why would I do that?"

"To get your ring back, maybe," Starla suggested.

"My ring? Of course I want that back. But I'm not going to break in to get it."

"Then why did you really come here if it wasn't to get the ring back?" Starla stared him down, her face turning red.

He shrugged, and the veins near his temples popped out. We'd caught him in a lie of some sort. "I was hoping if I couldn't convince you to start dating me again that I could convince you to give my ring back. It means a lot to me."

"I know you fed me some story about the ring being a family heirloom." Her eyes narrowed. "But I took it to a jeweler. He told me this wasn't antique. You lied to me."

His cheeks reddened. "It cost me a lot of money."

Now we were getting down to the truth of the matter.

"Look, I'm telling you that I did not break into a house to get the ring back. Yes, I do want it. I mean, I want to get back together with you even more. But I didn't think that was going to happen. I could really use my money back. I don't even have enough cash to pay my rent."

"But you had enough cash to fly out here?" Starla asked.

"I'll have you know that I had frequent flyer miles." His voice rose along with his temper.

"And what about the hotel where you're staying?"

"As a matter of fact, I'm not staying at a hotel yet," he said. "I was in Willie Wahoos all evening. Go ask anybody there."

"I will," Jackson said. "In the meantime, I'll take you down to the police station so you can have a nice, warm place to stay for the evening."

"What?" David began mouthing off as Jackson led him to the back of his SUV.

Jackson had one of his guys drive Starla and me back to my place. We only had an hour to change before the charity dinner, and both of us were still reeling from this afternoon's events.

Seeing David show up had just been weird.

As soon as we stepped into my house and had some privacy, I asked, "You doing okay?"

"I just can't believe he came here. I know he said he has an alibi, but it had to have been him who broke in last night. He's the only one who makes sense." Starla paused in the kitchen, a pouty frown on her face.

"Jackson will get to the bottom of it."

Starla's pout continued to grow, much like the Grinch's heart after he met Cindy Lou Who. "Dating him was a big mistake."

"We all make mistakes when it comes to love." I gently placed a hand on her arm.

Seeing her right now reminded me of how far I'd come. But I wasn't naïve enough to think that I'd now arrived and could never revert back to my old ways. Being here in Nags Head with Jackson kept me grounded.

"I know we do. But he just makes me so mad." She fisted her hands, her nostrils flaring.

This was not the mindset we needed to be in before the charity event this evening. It was unfortunate, to say the least.

"Look, why don't we get dressed and then we can

talk more tonight. The dinner will be a nice distraction from all of this, don't you think?"

"Yes, I do. It will be a nice distraction from everything."

Thirty minutes later, both Starla and I emerged dressed as . . . elves.

The Elf Extravaganza was going to be a blast. Tonight's events included a gingerbread house decorating contest, prizes for those in attendance, an auction, and a photo booth area.

People had paid fifty bucks a plate in order to eat with us. But the money would go one hundred percent to help buy presents for children who were less fortunate.

As we took a selfie together, something on the camera screen caught my eye.

There was someone on my deck.

Watching us.

CHAPTER
TWELVE

I STIFLED A SCREAM AND TURNED.

As I did, the figure fled.

"Someone was out there," I muttered.

Starla clutched my arm. "Should we chase him?"

"Only if we want to end up upside down in a chimney."

A pounding sounded at the door. I rushed toward it, peered out the peep hole, and spotted . . . Jackson.

Quickly, I took the locks off and let him inside. In one breath, I told him what had happened, about the shadowy figure outside.

"Stay here," he ordered.

As if I hadn't heard that a million times before. But I did as he asked.

I paced. I waited. I practiced my dance moves by doing the Floss.

Nervous habit. I was trying to break it.

Finally, Jackson appeared at the door again. A deep frown stained his face, and his breathing seemed heavier than usual, like he'd been running. "No one is there."

My heart sank with disappointment. Of course. That would have been too easy.

"Can you make out any details in the picture?" he asked.

"Great question. Let's go see."

Starla showed us the photo. But all we could see was a blurry image in the background.

What in the world was going on here? And how had Starla and I gotten involved?

I had no idea.

The Elf Extravaganza was a blast. Starla and I had decorated our gingerbread houses, which had then been auctioned off. We sang karaoke, ate tasty food, and mixed and mingled.

Thankfully Jackson was with us, providing security and a little eye candy.

Actually, he was so much more than eye candy, but I found it amusing to mentally call him that.

He was totally on guard duty today. If it wasn't

for the fleeting look of affection that I caught on occasion in his gaze, no one would guess we were engaged. He was all rigid lines and hyper focused as he kept his eyes open for any signs of danger. I actually found this side of him very attractive.

He'd even twirled me around the dance floor a few times, looking adorable in his ugly Christmas sweater. It only had snowflakes on it, so it was pretty tame. But I still loved it. I'd tried to talk him into wearing tiny beard lights, but he'd refused.

Our cameraman/producer wandered the crowds, filming everything. Three hours of film would probably boil down to thirty seconds of airtime.

Finally, it was time for Starla and me to go on stage for an auction. Annabelle was presiding over it. I couldn't help but survey everyone around us.

My gaze came to a stop on one of the men in the crowd. Why did he look familiar? I tried not to stare and to pull my gaze away, but I had definitely seen him somewhere before.

I searched my memories, trying to rewind them until I could come to a stop at the right place. If only it were that easy, or if my brain had some type of mental search capacity like all those police computers on TV.

Put in a picture and *voilà*! Two minutes later you had a match.

Unfortunately, my brain did not work that way. But something about the man bugged me.

I caught Jackson's gaze. He knew me well enough to read my body language and pick up on the fact that something was bothering me.

His gaze followed mine and stopped on the man. Then he looked back at me with another questioning look. I offered a slight shrug. I didn't know how else to communicate with him, considering that the camera was on and rolling.

Could that man be responsible for Christian Nolan's death? Had the killer himself come out to this event today just to keep an eye on this situation?

But it didn't make sense. Why would the killer be targeting Starla and me? Or had that been what this was about the whole time? Had the murder somehow been a ploy to reach out to me and Starla?

It seemed like a stretch. Then again, I'd seen a lot of other crazy things happen in the past. I didn't want to rule anything out yet.

CHAPTER
THIRTEEN

BEFORE I REALIZED what was happening, the auction ended.

I lost sight of Jackson and the mystery man.

Starla and I were ushered off stage as a local marching band took our places. An air of excitement zinged through the air. A couple students raised their hands for high fives. Nervous chatter sounded.

As a flurry of students filed past, Starla and I were separated.

I glanced across the sea of people toward her. It was no use. No way would I get through this crowd.

That's when I felt a tap on my shoulder.

I turned and saw Dasher standing there.

"I was hoping to catch you." He shoved his hands down into his pockets.

Did he have a gun there?

I sucked in a breath, at a loss for words.

He stared at me, almost looking confused. "I didn't mean to scare you. I just wanted to catch a moment alone with you."

I glanced behind me again. Where was Jackson?

"Why do you want a moment alone with me?"

"I was hoping you could help me."

I took a step back. "Do you really deliver luggage for the airport?"

A crease formed between his eyes. "Yes, of course."

"Did you follow me here?"

"I heard you'd be here and bought a ticket. Is that bad?"

"What do you want?" I took another step back.

"I was hoping you'd—"

Before he could finish, I heard a voice behind me. "Step away from Joey."

I didn't have to turn my head to recognize the voice.

Jackson.

He'd found me.

Thank goodness.

Dasher raised his hands and stepped back.

Jackson had that effect on people.

"I wasn't trying to start trouble," Dasher rushed.

Jackson wedged himself in front of me. "Then what were you trying to do?"

"I just wanted to know if my house could be featured on her show."

"What?" Jackson and I said at the same time.

Dasher nodded, his features softening. "I have a beautiful Christmas display, and I'd love to raise money for the Reindeer Riders."

"Reindeer Riders?" What in the world?

"Yeah, we're Santas, but on bikes. We deliver food to people who can't get out on Christmas. People don't always trust us because we're bikers."

"That's why you followed me?" I asked, still feeling dumbfounded.

"Yes. It would mean a lot to me to bring attention to our cause. We're trying to reform our image. I figured you'd know all about that."

Yes, I did know all about bouncing back from bad press. However, there wasn't a lot I could do for him in this case. "Sir, I'm sorry, but I don't pick the houses. The producers do, and I only do what they tell me to."

The hopeful expression left his gaze. "Oh, I see. I'm sorry. I thought it would be a great way to get some publicity for my charity."

"Why is the charity so important to you?"

"Because they helped out my mama when she

was sick." His eyes glossed over with emotion. "Now I want to help others also."

I glanced at Jackson. I wanted to argue with this man. I wanted to say his story couldn't possibly be true.

But of all the excuses he could have made . . . this one seemed to have too many details not to be true.

That left us back at square one.

I sighed.

***

After Dasher left, Jackson stepped closer. "I'm glad you're okay, but that could have been a lot different."

"I don't appear to be the target here," I reminded him. "Nolan was. Maybe the Curriers. Maybe even Starla. But not me."

"Maybe, but you always seem to be the focus."

"There are exceptions."

He let out a breathy chuckle and pulled me into a hug. "I just want you to be safe."

"I know."

We stepped away from each other.

"I think this whole case is weird," I said.

"Weirder than someone changing the script during your last movie?" Jackson raised his eyebrows.

"Yes. Maybe. In some ways. I mean, let's talk this through."

Jackson leaned against the wall and crossed his arms, settling in to listen.

"Nolan got out of jail, and one of the first things he did was devise a way to break into the Curriers' house. He was familiar with the place only because his friend used to live there. In fact, his friend lived there during the same time period when Nolan was robbing jewelry stores, even though the two had lost touch for a while."

"Correct."

I stood there in the hallway, working the details through in my mind. The band played "We Wish You a Merry Christmas" in the distance. Starla talked to our cameraman. Everything seemed surprisingly normal.

"But in the process of breaking into the Curriers' house, something happened. Someone saw it as an opportunity, hit him on the head, and stuck him in the chimney. He dies."

"Also correct."

"What we're trying—"

"What *I'm* trying," Jackson amended with a slight smile.

"What *you're* trying to figure out is why someone would kill him. Maybe this person was trying to get information from him on where this jewelry is."

"That's our best guess."

"Then you have to figure out who. Who would do this? Who knew about the jewelry? Who knew Nolan had gotten out? Who knew Nolan would be going to the Curriers' house that evening?"

"All great questions."

"Fitz was corresponding with Nolan and had some kind of weird fan boy thing going on. We don't know why he would kill him, but we do know he was deathly afraid of heights."

"Correct," Jackson said.

"Nolan's friend, who might be aware of Nolan hiding something in the Curriers' house, is dead. None of the jewelers Nolan robbed are suspects for various reasons. They would be the most obvious people."

"They would. But they're innocent. So . . ."

"Meanwhile, there was David, who just happened to wander back in town around the time all this was happening. I don't believe he has anything to do with Nolan's death. But was he the person who broke into my place and approached Starla?"

"His alibi seems pretty solid. He was definitely at Willie Wahoos. However, it would have probably only taken him twenty minutes to slip away and break into your place."

"I think you can rule the Puddingtons out," I continued.

"I agree."

"Annabelle did say Mr. Currier had a temper . . ."

"A lot of people do. That doesn't mean they're all killers."

"Also true." I let out a sigh. "If I were in your shoes, I'd have no idea where to look next."

"You can't rush these things. But we're doing our best."

I stepped closer and grabbed his lapels. "I know you are. Nags Head's finest is on the job."

His phone rang, and he put it to his ear. As he mumbled a few things, I tried to interpret them—unsuccessfully. When he ended the call, he looked over at me and frowned.

"What is it?"

"The Ryderz driver that took you home on the first night of filming? He's missing."

"What?" My hand went over my mouth. "That's terrible."

Jackson looked at something else on his phone and showed it to me. "He hasn't been heard from in two days."

I stared at the picture on the screen. "Jackson . . . that's not the guy who drove us."

He stared at me, not saying anything. But I knew what that meant.

If the Ryderz driver wasn't the right one, then Starla and I had likely been face to face with a killer.

CHAPTER
FOURTEEN

A POLICE OFFICER had been stationed outside of my house that night. Jackson wasn't even kidding when he told me to stay inside.

In the meantime, Starla and I had a Christmas parade to host this morning. After that, our stint with *Lit* would be done.

I'd never expected things to go like this.

At nine, Starla and I left to go to the school. Jackson's colleague drove us there.

"Where's Jackson?" I asked. I really thought he'd be here himself, and he hadn't answered when I'd tried his phone.

"He had something else he had to do."

Weird. I wondered what that might be.

The unease in my gut grew.

But I hardly had time to think about it. As soon as we arrived on site, everything was a blur of activity and instructions.

The next thing I knew, Starla and I were on our float with a "snow globe" around us. The snow globe was actually just plastic bars that had been bent to look like an orb.

The float was lovely, with a fake fireplace, two Christmas trees, and even stockings. The excitement in the air was contagious. This was going to be a great event. I only wished I didn't have this murder hanging over my head.

As the parade started, my phone rang. I tried not to look since I had people watching me. But when I saw Jackson's name, I knew I had to.

"I can't really talk," I whispered, still smiling at everyone around us.

"Joey, I went out to the prison today and interviewed Nolan's old cellmate."

"Great move on your part."

"It turns out Nolan admitted he'd worked with someone else when he robbed those jewelry stores," Jackson said. "He had a partner. He talked about it to his cellmate when he was in prison."

"And?" I knew there was more to this.

"I was able to track down a name and a picture," Jackson said. "I just texted it to you."

"One second." I glanced at my phone screen as the text message came in. When I saw the picture there, I gasped. "Jackson, that's the man who gave me and Starla a ride back to my house after that first night of filming."

I kept trying to smile and wave at the crowds, but my insides felt like a tornado was wreaking havoc.

"That's what I thought," Jackson said. "This guy's name is Eric Vadim. He's wanted for a slew of other crimes. Definitely not someone to be played with."

"Good to know." I had no intention of playing with him.

"We put an APB out for him. But I wanted to warn you. This guy obviously thinks that you and Starla are a threat somehow. It's the only reason he'd be targeting you right now."

"I'll be careful."

"I'm on my way to the parade now. Oh, and one more thing."

"What's that?" Did I really want to know?

"We found the actual Ryderz driver."

"Is he okay?"

"He is now. Apparently, he was running his mouth at the Christmas light filming, saying how excited he was to drive you and Starla around. This Eric guy lured him out of his car, told him his tire was going flat."

"That's horrible."

"Eric managed to knock the driver out and stowed him away in the trunk. He later dumped this guy in an unoccupied beach house. If the cleaning crew hadn't stopped by, we might have never found him. He was tied to a post and unable to move."

"That's terrible."

"Be careful, Joey."

"I will be."

I tried to concentrate on the parade. I really did. It was such a lovely event.

But my mind was on the case instead.

Nolan's partner, this Eric guy, must have realized where Nolan stashed that stolen jewelry. Maybe he'd followed Nolan after he'd been released from prison. Maybe he'd seen him go to the Curriers' house and realized the truth.

Something had happened to prevent him from getting the jewelry, though. Maybe he'd caught Nolan, threatened him, but Nolan still hadn't given up the location. He'd tortured him, hoping to force answers from him.

It still hadn't worked, and Nolan had died.

But Eric thought he had enough information to stick it out.

But what did that have to do with me and Starla?

I still wasn't sure.

"Smile, Joey," Starla muttered, still in beauty queen mode.

I widened my grin and smiled at people who'd lined the streets to watch the parade. A truck pulled us, and the rest of the floats followed, along with some horses, dance troops, and a marching band.

It was quite the event. Onlookers were dressed for Christmas, wore light up headbands, and cheered all around us from their spots on the sidewalk.

My gaze scanned the crowds.

If I were Eric Vadim, what would I do?

I knew.

I'd be here at the parade today, watching everything.

That did nothing to comfort me.

I continued to look around.

I didn't see him, though. Maybe I was reading too much into this.

We turned from the main highway and onto a side street. If I remembered correctly, we needed to loop back to the school.

As we did, a bike pulled up beside us.

I sucked in a breath.

It was him. Eric.

He rode on a bicycle beside us with a look of vengeance in his eyes.

CHAPTER
FIFTEEN

"STARLA, IT'S HIM!"

"What?" She gave me a confused look.

I supposed I hadn't told her the update yet.

"It's the man who killed Christian Nolan." My eyes were fixated on him as he stared at us. His bike hurtled through the crowds, knocking several onlookers from their seats. Cries of anger followed his path.

Starla gasped. "What are we going to do?"

That was a great question.

When I glanced at Eric again, I saw a gun tucked under his jacket.

Things had just turned ten times worse. Especially since there were so many innocent civilians around. Heck, *I* was an innocent civilian.

I had to tell Jackson.

For a moment, I forgot people were watching me. That I was supposed to be in a real-life snow globe. That I was supposed to represent.

Instead, I grabbed my phone and dialed Jackson's number.

"He's here," I blurted to Jackson.

"I'm only five minutes away."

"He has a gun, Jackson."

"Can you get into the truck that's pulling the float?"

I glanced at the truck bed in front of me. "I don't know . . . maybe."

"You're a sitting duck on the float. You need to take cover."

I couldn't agree more. "I'll see what I can do."

I ended the call and grabbed Starla's arm. "We've got to get on that truck."

"What?"

I looked at the man again. He still held his gun. I had no doubt he'd use it.

"How are we going to do *that?*" Starla's voice rose to a fever pitch.

"I have no idea. But if we walk to the edge of the platform and dive inside, it should work."

"Joey . . . this isn't what I signed up for." Her gaze flickered with fear.

"We don't have any other choice." I took her hand. "Come on."

She looked pensive, to say the least, as I led her toward the edge. The crowds around us watched, as if this was part of the show.

It wasn't.

The jump wasn't going to be as bad as I thought. Only a couple feet. Certainly we could make it.

I looked back at Eric and saw his gun now. It was aimed at us.

"Come on!" I yelled.

Before Starla could overthink it, I pulled her. We dove onto the truck.

As we did, I heard a bang. Glass broke.

I gasped.

The driver drifted into another lane.

That was when I realized what had happened.

The driver had been shot.

Eric had aimed at me or Starla but had missed. No one had heard the gunshot over the noise of the parade.

I glanced at our police escorts. How were they missing this?

I had to do something. Now.

Before there were more casualties.

Without thinking, I climbed through the small window at the back of the truck. The slider had been open and now half of it was broken. I avoided the jagged edges.

"Stay down!" I yelled at Starla. The last thing I wanted was for her to get hurt.

I shimmied into the truck in time to hear the driver moan.

He was still alive.

Thank goodness.

But blood stained his shoulder. He'd definitely been shot.

I glanced around. People were starting to notice. To cast each other concerned looks. Even the cops looked at each other.

Moving quickly, I climbed into the driver's seat. I apologized to the driver as I shoved in next to him. I had to reach the brakes and the steering wheel.

I veered back into the lane before anyone got hurt.

But I knew I had to get this guy away from the crowds. How was I going to do that?

Flinching, I made a split-second decision, praying for forgiveness as I did so.

I veered off the path, leading the biker away from the crowds—I hoped.

Around me, people gasped and screamed.

Dear Lord . . . what am I doing?

I prayed I didn't get anyone else hurt.

A crowd appeared in front of me, behind a makeshift barricade.

I gasped.

Where had they come from? Since this wasn't part of the parade route, the crowds must have gathered here.

This wasn't good.

I jerked the wheel to the right. In the process, I plowed into some Christmas inflatables in someone's yard.

I effectively ran over Santa and Frosty.

I glanced beside me again.

The man was still there. Still on his bike.

Still with a gun in hand.

Starla screamed in the back.

Holding my breath, I jerked the wheel again. This time, the truck rammed into Eric.

I prayed I'd made the right move.

I was about to find out.

CHAPTER
SIXTEEN

JUST AS I stepped out of the truck, I heard a familiar voice.

"Put your hands up!"

I looked over and saw Jackson. He'd gotten here just in time.

He stood with his gun drawn, pointed right at Eric.

Eric untangled himself from his bike and pulled himself up from the ground. With a scowl, he raised his hands.

Jackson kicked his gun away and another officer grabbed it. "Eric Vadim, you're under arrest."

"All I wanted was that stupid snow globe," he muttered.

Jackson jerked Eric's arms behind him and slapped on some handcuffs.

"The snow globe?" I said. "Is that what this has been about? We don't even have it with us."

"Yes I do, actually." Starla rose from the back of the truck. She picked up the bag she'd brought with her, reached inside, and pulled out the gift Fitz had given her. "I stuck it in here thinking maybe I'd get a picture with it. It would be great publicity."

"Someone broke into your house after you left for the parade," Jackson told me. "Everything has been gone through. Someone—Eric—was obviously looking for something."

Eric sneered but said nothing.

"May I?" Jackson handed Eric off to another officer and then extended his hand toward Starla.

She handed him the snow globe.

He took it and unscrewed the bottom. When he separated the two pieces, I peered over his shoulder and sucked in a breath. Inside was jewelry. Lots and lots of jewelry.

"This is where Nolan kept his secret stash," Jackson muttered.

"But Fitz gave that to me . . ." Starla sucked in a breath. "I don't understand."

"Nolan gave this snow globe to his friend knowing the family was a bunch of pack rats and wouldn't get rid of it. He didn't expect to be caught.

But as soon as he was released from prison, he went to the house trying to get the jewelry."

"I knew that's what he'd do!" Eric yelled. "I followed him."

"And you demanded that he tell you where the jewelry was," Jackson said.

"He wouldn't. I even threatened to leave him inside the chimney if he didn't. He didn't care."

"So you left him there to die?"

Eric shrugged. "Maybe."

"How did you know we had the jewelry in this snow globe?" I asked.

"I didn't, at first. I just wanted an inside look at the investigation, and that driver was the easiest connection I could find. Then I saw that guy give you the snow globe. I'd seen Nolan buy that. Everything suddenly made sense."

"You broke into our house to retrieve it," I said. "That was *you* that night. Fitz really did scare you off."

"I just want what's rightfully mine."

"But you guys stole this jewelry," Jackson said. "It never belonged to you."

Eric sneered again.

"What about the man you said you saw on the first night of filming?" I asked. "Who was he?"

His sneer turned into a sickening grin. "I made him up just to waste your time."

Jackson shook his head, not bothering to hide his disgust. "Take him away." As an officer led Eric away, Jackson turned to me. "Are you okay?"

I nodded. "I'm fine. But the driver . . ."

I looked back and saw paramedics treating him. Thank goodness.

I scanned everything around me, remembering the parade and how everything might have come across. The whole procession had come to a halt. People gawked. Cameras snapped pictures.

But at least everyone was safe now.

"Those were some moves you had back there." Jackson's eyes sparkled as he stepped closer to me. "Just like one of your movies."

I shrugged. "I had no idea what I was doing. I just knew I had to do something."

"You did good, Joey."

"You really did," Starla agreed.

"Thanks. I'm just sorry it all happened."

"It looks like you saved Christmas," Jackson said.

I stared at the horrified crowds. The confused float participants behind us. And Annabelle as she rushed our way.

Finally, my gaze stopped on the deflated Santa I'd plowed over.

I frowned. "Or I wrecked it."

The next day, I turned to Starla as she waited for her ride to the airport. "I'm so glad you came."

She threw her arms around me. "I am too, Joey. It was great seeing you in this environment. It suits you."

"You think?"

She nodded. "I think."

"Thanks."

Her smile disappeared a little. "It made me a little envious, truth be told."

"Why's that?"

She shrugged and stared off into the distance. "I'm in the rat race, I guess. It's a different kind of rat race than most people. It's the Hollywood rat race. I always feel like I'm competing with people, trying to get the most attention."

"But you're doing so great."

"I keep getting passed up for roles. I've even heard that I'm getting too old or that I need to lose some weight. My star power is diminishing, and I'm not handling it well. It's one of the reasons I talked you into doing this with me. I wanted some of your goodness to rub off on me."

"Oh, Starla . . ."

"It's true. It's why I dated David—just for the attention. It's why I recorded Jackson chasing down someone outside your house. I want the online clout. But you don't seem to be chasing those things anymore."

"I have my moments, but I've come a long way. It's much more fun when things chase you." I paused. "Except killers. No one wants killers chasing them."

"Maybe I'll get there one day."

"I'm sure you will. Any time you need, come out to visit. Maybe getting away will help. It did for me."

"Maybe I'll do that." The SUV pulled up, and Starla gave me another hug. "Thanks again. I'm so happy for you and Jackson. You've got a good one."

"I know I do. Thanks."

She climbed inside as the driver put her luggage in the back. Before closing the door, she called, "Merry Christmas!"

"Merry Christmas to you too!"

As they pulled away, Jackson stepped out of my house with a peppermint mocha in his hands. He handed me the warm drink and wrapped his arms around my waist.

"Another week, another adventure with Joey," he murmured in my ear.

"I promise I don't look for trouble."

"I know you don't. It's just that most people deck the halls . . ."

"And I wreck them. I know." I took a sip of my drink before frowning.

"It doesn't change how much I love you."

I turned in his arms until we faced each other. "That's the best Christmas gift of all."

A smile stretched across his face before he leaned toward me and planted a soft kiss on my lips.

Yes—all was merry and bright.

~~~

Thank you so much for reading *Wreck the Halls*. If you enjoyed this book, please consider leaving a review!

Keep reading for a preview of *Glitch and Famous*.

GLITCH AND FAMOUS: CHAPTER ONE

As Jackson Sullivan and I stood facing each other in the middle of my kitchen, it felt like the two of us were the only ones who existed. Kind of like Kate Winslet and Idris Elba in *The Mountain Between Us*.

Except they were in the mountains trying to survive perilous conditions, and Jackson and I were at my beach house trying to navigate wedding planning.

Despite the horrible comparison, I *would* love to freeze this moment. My doors and windows were open, and the fresh scent of salty ocean floated through the screens. The aroma of the chicken chili I'd ordered for lunch still lingered in the air—probably because I hadn't fully cleaned up from the meal. And my coconut-infused shampoo seemed to be the cherry on top of the scent-o-rama paradise.

And then there was Jackson, the most perfect leading man I'd ever met. The next few weeks were going to be totally dedicated to planning my wedding to this man.

And nothing was going to deter me.

Nothing.

Jackson gently pushed a lock of hair behind my ear as he gazed at me like Romeo gazed at Juliet—except neither of us had ended up dead.

Not yet.

Man, I was on a roll thinking of awful couples to compare us with.

"I'm glad you're back home," Jackson murmured. "I've missed you, Joey."

I ran my hand across his cheek, soaking in every inch of his handsome face—from his blue eyes to the stubble across his cheeks, chin, and upper lip.

I'd missed Jackson more than I ever thought was possible. As I gazed at him, my heart felt so full of love that I hardly knew what to do with it all.

I could plan a production, complete with song and dance. Announce the state of my heart online for all to see. Jump on a couch while speaking with Oprah.

So many choices.

None of which I would employ.

Not right now, at least.

Instead, I'd enjoy this moment.

"I've missed you too, Jackson." I scooted closer to him—close enough that, if I leaned in, I caught a whiff of his leathery cologne. "I don't ever want to be away from you for that long again."

I'd just finished filming the newest season of *Relentless*, my TV show, *and* a movie. Though Jackson and I had seen each other on some weekends and on breaks between filming, it hadn't been the same. I wanted to do life together with him, and that wasn't how our schedules had meshed lately.

But now I was back in the oceanside house I'd bought in Nags Head, North Carolina, and I didn't plan on going anywhere for a long time. Spring was the perfect time to enjoy this area with its mild weather, windswept beaches, and awesome seafood.

Jackson leaned back, his fingers still tangled in my hair.

I wasn't complaining. As long as I was close to him, I was as happy as James Cameron at the Oscars after *Titanic* won.

"So, you want to tell me something?" Jackson asked.

I frowned. There was one problem to my total dedication to wedding planning . . .

"Lennon asked to stay a couple more days," I blurted.

Jackson squinted. "I thought she was just here overnight?"

"She was . . . but she likes it so much that she hinted she might like to stay, so . . ." I twisted my lips in a frown.

"You offered to let her stay."

"I did. I'm sorry. I know we were supposed to do some wedding planning. We still can."

Lennon Seagram, an old friend—more of an acquaintance really—had arrived in town last night to visit me. Jackson had been working a robbery when she arrived, a job that bled into this morning and afternoon.

Now, just as Jackson had been able to stop by after his shift, Lennon had gone for a quick walk.

"Why exactly is she here? Were you two really close?"

Jackson's question was valid. It wasn't like I'd talked to him about Lennon before.

I sucked on my bottom lip, contemplating how to answer without sounding rude. "We've never been super close, but we're friends. Besides, they say salt-water heals all wounds. I want other people to experience how amazing fresh air and sunshine can be. If I can give them a moment of the solitude I had when I first came—"

"I think your memories and mine are totally

different," Jackson interrupted, his eyes narrowed. "I don't remember any kind of solitude when you moved here. In fact, I seem to remember everything suddenly becoming much more complicated and a trail of trouble following you wherever you went."

"Maybe on the outside things were complicated. But on the inside—" I tapped my heart dramatically. I *was* an actress, so drama was kind of my thing "—everything clicked in place. Especially when I met you."

A grin stretched across his handsome face. "You know just what to say, don't you?"

I shrugged, feeling smug. "I do have a way with words, if I say so myself."

"Do you know what else you have a way with?" Jackson raised his eyebrows.

"No. Why don't you remind me?"

He leaned toward me again and pressed his lips against mine. But this was no quick peck. This was a kiss that could consume me like the ocean consumed the *Titanic*.

Except that ended in tragedy.

Why was I still thinking about James Cameron?

This was a kiss that could consume me like a little kid set loose in a candy shop.

Except eating that many sweets was *so* unhealthy.

I needed to try again.

This was a kiss that could consume me like—

Before I could figure out the perfect way to describe it, I heard the front door open.

I pulled away from Jackson and sighed. One day, the two of us really would have some alone time— some *quality* alone time. In fact, I looked forward to having the rest of our lives together.

But for now, I had a guest to entertain.

"Come on." I stepped back and took his hand. "This has to be Lennon. Let me introduce the two of you."

Before we reached the front door, I spotted someone crumpled on the entryway floor.

I gasped.

Lennon.

She raised her head, and I saw tears pouring from her eyes. Her white-blonde hair looked disheveled, one eye was swollen, and her knees were bloody.

Jackson and I sprinted toward her, kneeling on either side of her.

"Lennon?" I rushed. "What happened?"

Lennon looked up, her moisture-filled blue eyes consumed with pain and panic. "Please. Help me. I was just . . . attacked."

Click here to continue reading.

ALSO BY CHRISTY BARRITT:

ABOUT THE AUTHOR

USA Today has called Christy Barritt's books "scary, funny, passionate, and quirky."

Christy writes both mystery and romantic suspense novels that are clean with underlying messages of faith. Her books have sold more than three million copies and have won the Daphne du Maurier Award for Excellence in Suspense and Mystery, have been twice nominated for the Romantic Times Reviewers' Choice Award, and have finaled for both a Carol Award and Foreword Magazine's Book of the Year.

She is married to her Prince Charming, a man who thinks she's hilarious—but only when she's not trying to be. Christy is a self-proclaimed klutz, an avid music lover who's known for spontaneously bursting into song, and a road trip aficionado.

When she's not working or spending time with her family, she enjoys singing, playing the guitar, and exploring small, unsuspecting towns where people have no idea how accident-prone she is.

Find Christy online at:
www.christybarritt.com
www.facebook.com/christybarritt
www.twitter.com/cbarritt

Sign up for Christy's newsletter to get information on all of her latest releases here: **www.christybarritt. com/newsletter-sign-up/**

facebook.com / AuthorChristyBarritt
twitter.com / christybarritt
instagram.com / cebarritt

Made in the USA
Las Vegas, NV
24 April 2024

89085504R00100